A gentle knock sounded. Beck fought down the rush of excitement and opened the door calmly. "Hello, May."

She looked beautiful—when did she not?—and walked past him into the room. She wore a sexy black off-shoulder top that left her firm midriff bare, and a fire-engine-red clingy short skirt that hugged her hips adoringly.

He'd invited her in for research. *Right.*

"Thanks for coming."

"I haven't yet, but you're welcome." Smiling, May faced him, and whatever uncertainty had been plaguing her before was gone. She was on fire, eyes bright and sure.

"Uh, would you like a drink first—"

She held up a hand to stop him. "Let's just do it, Beck."

Her soft words had the opposite effect on his arousal. He needed to focus on the scene playing out before him, focus on his book. He grabbed his laptop. "Mind if I take notes?"

"Knock yourself out."

She stood still for a second. Putting her hands on the hem of the shirt, she lifted it slowly, exposing full round breasts captured—barely, it seemed—in a few inches of sheer black lace, nipples clearly visible under the sheer fabric.

Beck's hands froze on the keyboard. *Oh, my.*

Blaze™

Dear Reader,

Who wouldn't want to be treated to a week in a luxury boutique hotel in Manhattan? Especially a "discreet" hotel like Hush, where anything goes and the staff is trained to lift no eyebrows and refuse no request.

My heroine, small-town girl May Ellison, rebounding from the only relationship she's ever had, thinks this is not a bad idea either, especially once she meets sexy celebrity author Beck Desmond. During her week at Hush, May gets to indulge herself at the spa, pool, library, restaurant and a certain unusually titillating bar....

Welcome to the fabulous miniseries, DO NOT DISTURB, brought to you by yours truly and some of my favorite Harlequin Blaze authors. We worked closely together to create this fabulous fantasy place. Want a virtual visit? Go to www.hushhotel.com and check yourself in. Can't get enough? Spend time at www.eHarlequin.com as the series' books come out, and look for each author's bonus short story, set in one of Hush's rooms. You can also chat with the authors on the site and ask us questions!

Finally, don't miss the excerpt from the next DO NOT DISTURB story, *Kiss & Makeup* by Alison Kent, at the end of this book.

Hope you enjoy May and Beck's adventure and the miniseries! Let me know. You can e-mail me through my Web site, www.IsabelSharpe.com.

Cheers,

Isabel Sharpe

ISABEL SHARPE
Thrill Me

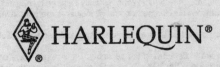

HARLEQUIN®

TORONTO • NEW YORK • LONDON
AMSTERDAM • PARIS • SYDNEY • HAMBURG
STOCKHOLM • ATHENS • TOKYO • MILAN • MADRID
PRAGUE • WARSAW • BUDAPEST • AUCKLAND

To Tracy Miller,
who has brought so much happiness to those I love best

ISBN 0-373-79190-9

THRILL ME

Copyright © 2005 by Muna Shehadi Sill.

This edition published by arrangement with Harlequin Books S.A.

® and TM are trademarks of the publisher. Trademarks indicated with
® are registered in the United States Patent and Trademark Office, the
Canadian Trade Marks Office and in other countries.

www.eHarlequin.com

Printed in U.S.A.

1

MEMORANDUM

To: Staff
From: Janice Foster, General Manager, HUSH Hotel
Date: Sunday, July 6
Re: Trevor Little

Mr. Trevor Little will be bringing another guest this week. We will be following the usual pattern of gifts: flowers Monday, spa visit Tuesday, bracelet Wednesday, negligee Thursday and the molded chocolate sculpture Friday. Reminder: please treat his guest with absolute courtesy and do not act as if you've seen him here before. As usual, calls to his room should be forwarded to his voice mail and anyone asking for him should be told he is not registered here.

Note on housekeeping board:

Someone else gets to clean Trevor Little's room. I got it last time. Yick!

IF SHE THOUGHT of the Midwest Airlines airplane as a womb, and the jetway into Newark airport as a birth canal, then May Hope Ellison figured she was about to be reborn. Her first symbolic breaths of new life were only yards away in the hallowed area outside gate B40.

Okay, so maybe that was pushing it.

She'd been planning to fly into LaGuardia since Manhattan was her destination, but Trevor had insisted she fly into Newark. To save her the traffic and hassle of LaGuardia, he'd said. And with luck, he'd get out of his meeting in New Jersey early and be able to meet her on the eleven-thirty-five train to Penn Station.

May's mother, born and bred in Wisconsin, but lived in the Big Apple for a couple of years before she married, had shrugged and said *she'd* never had any trouble at LaGuardia.

Of course May hadn't told her mother about Trevor. Mom thought May was exploring New York with her high school friend Ginny. Mothers didn't generally get very excited about daughters flying halfway across the country to spend a week of wild passion in a luxury boutique hotel with a man they barely knew.

Well, maybe they did get excited. But not in a good way.

One more step, around the corner, and there was her first sight of her new temporary life and— Wow. Lots of gates. Lots of noise. Lots and lots of people. This was not Milwaukee. And it certainly wasn't Oshkosh.

She wasn't aware she'd stopped dead until someone bumped into her and muttered something not terribly flattering or polite.

Forward, then, going with the flow, heading out of the gate-studded cul-de-sac, up a long corridor, then around another corner into the main terminal. Even more people. Security lines many many yards long, three of them, two and three people deep. She clutched the directions Trevor had e-mailed her and followed signs for the shuttle to the N.J. Transit train that would take her into the city.

After much confusion, buying the wrong ticket to the wrong destination—*why* would they name both the New York and New Jersey stations Penn Station?—she finally made it onto the right train, counting the cars carefully so she'd be in the one she and Trevor agreed upon. Third behind the engine.

Unfortunately, he wasn't there. Or fortunately, depending on whose nerves you asked. Not that she wasn't thrilled to be doing this, of course she was. It's just that…well how did you behave during a long commute with someone you barely knew that you were planning to screw for an entire week?

Hey, how are you? Hot for this time of year, isn't it? Looking forward to penetrating me?

Maybe it was better they'd meet at the hotel.

Half an hour later, May emerged from the train onto a hot, dark, underground platform, dragging her rolling suitcase behind her. She inched along, in closer proximity to more strangers than she cared to be, and struggled up the stairs. Penn Station made Newark Airport look like a ghost town.

Not that she'd never seen crowds before. Not that she hadn't expected everything to be Milwaukee times four, Oshkosh times ten. And Pine River, Wisconsin, the town she grew up in, times…did they make numbers that big?

Onward to her adventure. She'd met Trevor a month ago when he'd come through for the University of Wisconsin "spirit day" celebration and stopped by to catch up with an old professor at the business school, where she worked as assistant to the Dean.

They'd hit it off immediately. Gone from polite chat, to his invitation for coffee, to his invitation to drinks, to his invitation to dinner, to his invitation to his hotel room, which she'd declined, though she'd been tempted. When had any man paid this much attention to her? Then after he left town, he'd e-mailed her. Called her. And, incredibly, called her again. Until chatting with him became a regular part of her day. A bright spot in the last few dismal months since Dan had pronounced their six-year relationship over, because he wasn't feeling the excitement anymore. Because he'd had a vision of them together for the rest of their lives, doing the same things, having the same arguments they'd had since college, and it wasn't pretty.

Pretty? Who could keep pretty going forever? Life wasn't an adventure day in and day out. You worked, you came home, you had kids, you raised them, you retired, you died. Along the way you found things to enjoy so you stayed out of ruts.

Of course she couldn't stop him going where he needed to go. But feeling left behind sucked, not to mention feeling as if your guts had been ripped out. Though she knew Dan top to bottom, and couldn't help the sneaking suspicion that after he sowed whatever oats he felt he had to sow, he'd be back and their lives would progress smoothly toward the future as they'd always planned. Life was beautiful and miraculous all on its own. You didn't need to keep creating adrenaline rushes to enjoy it.

Okay, so she *was* after one now. Probably in reaction to what Dan had said about her, about their lives to-

gether. Dull and predictable? Not this week, honey. The
e-mails and phone calls with Trevor had gotten increasingly intimate. Increasingly…sexual in tone. Why not?
Dan was the only man she'd ever been with, and admittedly she was curious. Trevor was extremely attractive,
and he must be a gazillionaire because he'd unexpectedly and thrillingly invited her to stay with him for a
week at HUSH Hotel in Manhattan.

Her jaw had nearly hit her desk when she researched
it on Google and got an eyeful of the luxurious accom-
modations, the "discreet" nature of the place. Said jaw
nearly hit the floor when she got a load of the price tag.
A family of four could eat for a month on what it cost
to stay there one night.

So here she was, on her way to having a wild, wonderful sexual fling. And then going back to her so-called
boring life. Which didn't really seem that boring apart
from a little restlessness, a niggling suspicion now and
then that there must be more. She figured that was normal. Her mom had chased a dream to Radio City Music
Hall and discovered being a Rockette was hard work,
fun, sometimes tedious, occasionally exciting, occasionally disappointing, same as anything. Maybe
that's what Dan needed to learn. Maybe once he learned
it, he'd come back to her.

Or maybe this week would change everything.

Now. To find her way up to street level and get a taxi
to the hotel. She moved purposefully forward and
bumped into someone, then someone else on the re-
bound. "Excuse me, I'm sor—"

"Watch where you're going, honey."

Honey? She made a face at the suited back of the re-
treating jerk, and then realized poking her tongue out

in Penn Station was definitely not a New Yorker thing to do. Giving him the finger probably was, but she didn't have that in her.

Okay. She was going to have to become Veronica Lake to deal with this. All her life she'd combated shyness and introvert tendencies that separated her from the social mainstream. As a tactic to give herself courage she'd imitated leading ladies from her mother's stack of old movies. When Mom said she looked like Veronica Lake, her movie star persona had achieved focus.

So. Onward, Veronica.

She straightened and walked briskly, trying not to gawk at everything, trying to keep a furtive eye out for signs to where she was going. Seventh Avenue, Eighth Avenue, which exit did she want?

She picked Seventh and was rewarded with a street view and the marquis of Madison Square Garden. Taxi stand here, Trevor had said. Yes, there. With a thirty-foot lineup.

Veronica's who-cares expression crumpled a little. Was everyone in New York waiting here? It would take hours to get a cab.

Straightening her shoulders, she marched to the end of the line. No problem. Veronica did this all the time. This was her city. She was coming home after a wild weekend with fraternity boys at Princeton. Nobody better mess with her.

In line, she started realizing how warm it was for early July, at least compared to Oshkosh. The noon sun managed to find its way through the buildings and beat right down on her. Horns honked. The whistle of the uniformed man guiding people to cabs shrieked repeatedly. Cigarette smoke traveled unerringly into May's face with every puff and exhale of the woman in front of her. Sweat formed on her forehead and prickled under her arms. Lovely. She hoped she had the chance to shower at the hotel before Trevor showed up.

A thrill of adrenaline shot through her as she moved up in the line. She was really doing this. Really going to see him again. Really going to spend the week in his jovial sexy presence. Really going to have the kind of attention and luxury lavished on her that most people only dreamed about.

Hot damn.

Except as she moved closer—and no, she wasn't going to have to wait for hours, duh farm girl—the adrenaline kept coming, but the thrill turned more to fear. The woman in front of her lit another cigarette. The sun kept shining on May's too-heavy jacket. A cab farther back in line tried to take on a fare before his turn and the man with the whistle blew shrilly and kept blowing, then held up the line for five eternal sweaty smoky minutes by having a...well, *animated* shall we say, conversation with the driver.

People around her muttered. A drunk passed, yelling randomly about Jesus and video games and roast pork sandwiches.

Then it was May's turn. The cab pulled up. She lugged her suitcase in and sat, registering disappointment at the non-air-conditioned interior.

The driver glanced in his rearview mirror with dark tired eyes. "Where to?"

She gave him her haughtiest movie star stare while her entire body begged her to tell him to drive her back to Wisconsin, damn the cost.

"Hush Hotel."

His brows shot up, he turned fully around and—oh

joy—leered at her, then winked and pulled out into heavy-but-moving traffic. And for the next fifteen minutes, while the meter ticked higher at a speed faster than his, he proceeded to try as hard as he could to get them into a fatal accident.

My God, the city was immense, impossibly crowded, a hodgepodge of neat and slovenly storefronts and neat and slovenly people. How could anyone stand having to navigate all this every day? No wonder New Yorkers were considered tough. You needed a thick protective coating just to cross the street.

Finally, the driver executed another of his who-needs-lanes moves, pulled under the overhang in front of the hotel and came to a stop that made the whole car bounce. "Here you go."

May fumbled shakily in her wallet. How much was too much to tip? How much wasn't enough? She erred on the side of too much. After all, he'd done his best to teach her how precious her life was.

He accepted the bills with a nod. May took a deep breath. Three, two, one—

The door to the cab opened, and an attractive man in a black uniform with silver buttons and HUSH stitched in pink letters on the left breast of his jacket extended a white-gloved hand to help her out.

She took it reluctantly and emerged into the exhaust-smelling air to a hot breeze that threatened her careful French twist. Her head started to throb.

"Good afternoon, ma'am. Welcome to Hush Hotel."

A sudden burst of jackhammering in the street made him have to shout.

She nodded cool thanks, not wanting to have to shout back, and nodded again to the other attractive black-uniformed man who whisked her bag out of the cab behind her. Should she tip all these people? How much? God she was out of her depth.

The jackhammer clattered again. Another young hunky hotel employee blew his whistle for another cab. Someone shouted behind her. An ambulance siren grew louder; horns honked frantically as cars tried to get out of its way. May did manage to resist the urge to launch herself into the hotel through the ornate leaded-glass doors, but probably walked a bit quicker toward them than was perfectly *haute*-whatever of her.

A massive-shouldered doorman whooshed open the door just as she reached it and was about to put out her hand. She stepped inside and immediately wished she was somebody Terribly Important, and that she had a Terribly Chic faux-fur wrap to slip from her shoulders into the waiting arms of an attendant. Then she'd burst into a sultry song and the uniformed men around her would be her dancing chorus.

What a place.

Cool air wafted through the midsized lobby, deliciously scented with something vaguely herbal she couldn't identify. A few people milled about, a few checking in or out, a few in consultation with the pink-haired concierge. A few sitting in deep comfortable-looking black-and-grey or seafoam green chairs. Few being the operative word.

Best of all? Quiet. Who put the hush in HUSH Hotel? Whoever did, May's head was extremely grateful. And her nerves even more so. The tension started ebbing out of her. She half expected to leave a visible stress trail as she walked over the lush carpet—

black, gray, pink and touches of that lovely green—
following the bellhop up to the registration desk, a
chest-high shiny black lacquer rectangle. Behind it on
the wall in pink neon, the word HUSH, in art deco lettering.

Oh, this was *soooo* cool.

May gave her name, affecting bored disinterest,
while willing her cheeks not to flush as she did so. *Hi,
I'm May Hope Ellison, I'm here to have sex for an entire week with someone I barely know.*

Of course she needn't have worried. The registration
was speedy and pleasant. The lovely woman behind the
counter couldn't have been more professionally cor-
dial. Did anyone ugly work in this hotel?

With a nod of her perfectly coiffed head toward the
elevator and a genuine smile along with the key card,
the-lovely-woman-behind-the-counter sent May off to
her den of iniquity, hunky bellhop in tow, past more
chairs, a mirror and a black cat with a pink collar, which
no one but her seemed surprised to see sauntering about
the lobby.

Waiting for the elevator, May kept her face impassive, legs practically quivering from suppressed anxiety. As the doors closed in front of her face, and the
bellhop lit the fourteenth-floor button pink, her panic
rose. She needed a time-out. A moment for a deep
breath. Or twenty. But how could she tell this lovely, patient, suitcase-bearing Adonis that she was completely
freaking out?

She couldn't.

Ten…eleven…twelve…fourteen, and here they
were. She stepped out of the elevator and stared blindly
at the room number directions painted on the wall. Her

room was number 1457. Which direction did that mean? Her brain was gone. Liquefied. Soon it would seep out of her ears and that would be that.

Adonis cleared his throat, gestured to the left. May smiled and thanked him, grateful when her tight voice didn't crack. She really didn't want him there if she opened the door to Trevor. Didn't want anyone to bear witness to her nervous meltdown. But what choice did she have? She didn't have Dan and his calm, protective, take-charge strength to go back to. She was on her own.

Sally forth. She reached 1457, thrust the key card into the lock. Green light went on. Door opened. May went in.

Empty.

She took a few more steps in; the bathroom door was open.

Empty, too.

Oh, thank God.

A rush of delighted relief made her bestow a giant smile of gratitude on Adonis and give him five dollars, which in her estimation was a ridiculously enormous tip but for him probably branded her as Cowpoke Cathy.

He accepted the cash, gave a slight bow and exited the room.

So.

Panic over, she turned to survey her home for the next week. In a word: *exquisite*. A king-size bed with an arched headboard of two-toned wood, cherry and maple, dominated the room. She sank onto the thick down comforter in geometric patterns of black, white and burgundy. Bliss. She lay flat, her no-longer-aching head relishing the soft pillows, then stretched her right arm over the empty side, imagining Trevor lying there.

Along with the thrill of anticipation came an unexpected stab of nervous pain and longing for Dan. She put her hand to her chest where his grandmother's locket had rested for so many years. It still felt empty.

Enough. She sat up abruptly, padded over the thick cream carpet with a burgundy border, past the elegant spare desk that echoed the two-toned wood of the bed. On it, a bouquet of white and burgundy alstroemeria reflected the colors in the room; the feathery greens added a fresh, living contrast. On a slender-legged table near the window stood a giant bouquet of at least two dozen red roses. With a card. "I can't wait to see you. Trevor."

She smiled and rubbed the edge of the card back and forth across her chin. Dan was in the past—and possibly again in her future someday. But he didn't exist to her here. This would be a really, really nice week.

She drew back the gauze curtains and gazed out at the cityscape, at the people hurrying along the sidewalk. It was so peaceful away from all that rush and chaos. She let the curtain fall.

What else? Drawing back the doors on the entertainment center exposed a TV twice the size of hers at home, a VCR, a DVD player and in a narrow cabinet, video-recording equipment.

Gulp.

To the left, a black lacquer tray displaying fancy bottled water, glasses and ice. A bowl of apples, clementines, kiwis and grapes, and a basket of rolls and crackers. In the minibar along with the usual assortment of booze and snacks, lay foil-wrapped French cheese, pâté and tins of smoked oysters.

Oh, this was so not what she was used to. Ginny would freak. May would have to take careful note of everything to report back to her glamour and celebrity-hungry friend. What heaven. At least for a while. Eventually it, too, would get dull and predictable, like everything familiar.

In the bathroom she discovered a huge whirlpool tub, a portable showerhead, a bathrobe, a beautifully arranged basket of high-end cosmetics, lotions, shampoo and specialty soaps—all a hell of a lot fancier than the stuff she bought from the Pick 'n Save in Oshkosh.

Total fantasy. Impulsively, she turned on the tub and left it filling. That's what she needed. A nice soak to get rid of the travel smells, the city smells and the cigarette smoke smell that still clung to her from the woman in line at the cabstand. To refresh herself.

And if Trevor showed up in the middle of it, so much the better.

She smiled wickedly, went back into the room to undress and noticed the message light blinking on the black-and-gold old-fashioned style phone. She punched the button and unpinned her French twist. Receiver pressed against her cheek, she shook her head to let her long hair flow past her shoulders, wicked smile turned dreamy.

The machine picked up; the message played. Trevor's voice.

She listened. Hit Replay when the computerized voice gave her the option, and listened again. Just in case she hadn't heard right the first time. Just in case the second time through would be different.

It wasn't.
Trevor wasn't coming.

MEMORANDUM

To: Staff
From: Janice Foster, General Manager, HUSH
Hotel
Date: Monday, July 7
Re: Beck Desmond

Most of you already know that we are hosting author Beck Desmond in 1217. I'm posting another reminder that he is not to be approached for autographs or chitchat. While strolling the various parts of the hotel, he is often deep in concentration and we don't want to be responsible for interfering with his work. It's an honor that he's chosen HUSH as inspiration for the setting of his next thriller. Anyone who bothers him will be transferred immediately to the pet area for waste removal duty.

Note for Shandi Fossey, bartender, Erotique:

*See if you can get me Beck Desmond's autograph.
Janice*

BECK DESMOND took the phone away from his ear and stared at it with immense irritation. From the black receiver emerged the shrill heavily New York–accented voice of his agent, Alex Barkhauser, chattering away. He felt like affecting a high thin voice and saying, "Yes, dear" at regular intervals.

Except that was undoubtedly what she wanted him to do.

After a deep breath, he put the receiver back to his ear. Might be a good idea to hear at least some of what she was saying.

"…me wrong here, Beck, your books are great, you know they're great and you know I love them. But I just feel…"

He pictured her squinting off to one side, gesturing in swooping circles the way she always did, as if she were beckoning the words out of her mouth. "Yes?"

"I just feel like we're sitting on something that could get bigger, you know?"

"Bigger." He let the word drop, then waited. Old sales technique his father taught him; let the silence sit and your opponent will fill it with what you need to know.

"Sharon and I think you should try more emotion in your stories, more warmth, add a girlfriend for Mack, soften him up a little. Believe me, you'll double your readership. Women will buy you in droves. Right now you're selling to men. Women are a huge market in book sales. Huge. This is the next big step in your career."

Beck leaned back in the chair he'd brought with him from his condo on East 97th Street, spanned his temples with his thumb and middle finger and squeezed to try and relieve the ache. "Let me get this straight. You want me to take my hero, Mack, who has seen more of the baseness of human nature than anyone alive, and—"

"Soften him up. Give him more heart. Give him more sensitivity. Give him…"

"A puppy?"

He heard a sharp thwack, and knew Alex had slammed her palm on the desk, a sure sign his complete joke of an idea excited her. "Yes! Perfect! A puppy. Small one, the kind women love to stop and pat in the street. He could meet his—"

"You've got to be kidding me, Alex." Next she'd want Beck's ruthless detective spending afternoons shopping for shoes. "Mack is a man. No, he's more than that, he's *the* man."

"So make him *the* man with *the* woman."

"I can't."

"Why?"

"Because he's a loner, he's a tough guy. It's not him."

"Give him a woman strong enough to change him."

"Strong enough to—" Beck reached for his bottle of Evian water and found his fingers trying to strangle it. Change him? Change the man Beck had lived with in his imagination for seven years, through more harrowing adventures, more near-fatal experiences, more death-defying risks than any mere mortal could stand? The man who'd taken down serial killers, drug lords, crime bosses, international art thieves, muggers, murderers and everything between? *Change* him? With a *woman?* "I thought women knew never to get involved with a man hoping to change him."

"She can change him without trying. Simply by being who she is and affecting him that way. Having him become a better person because of loving her."

"The only effect I want any woman to have on Mack is a raging hard-on. I don't write romance novels."

Alex made the sound of exasperation New Yorkers excelled at, a cross between a cough and a raspberry. "I'm not *asking* you to write a romance novel. Just make him more human."

Beck exhaled his annoyance. The very quality that

made Alex Barkhauser an incredibly effective agent on his behalf, also made her a formidable opponent. Namely, she was a pit bull. "I'm sorry, I can't see Mack—"

"Here's an example." Pages rustled over the line. "The sex scene you have here with whatsername."

"Tamara."

"Tamara." Alex's voice turned scornful. "Total stripper name. Call her Susie or something."

"Susie? Susie wears pigtails and scuffed sandals, not black lingerie. And women named Susie don't masturbate."

"Well no woman masturbates like this."

"Like what?" The defensive edge in his voice disgusted him.

"Like a male fantasy from a porn movie."

Beck's mouth opened to protest. Then closed. Because it had nothing to say. That's exactly what had inspired the scene. A movie he'd snuck in to see as a teenager and had never forgotten.

"You can't tell me your girlfriends do it like that when they're alone. Wearing this entire black lace getup, do you have any idea how itchy and uncomfortable that stuff is? Plus, you have to be five-eleven, one hundred and ten pounds but oh, yes, somehow with enormous boobs, to look good in it. And the ten-inch dildo? Please."

"Alex. Can we move on to—"

"Make it more real, Beck. That's what I'm saying. The book rocks otherwise. But make Mack's relationship with women, his attention to women, his sex with women, more real. Less like a teenage boy's wet dream. Let's start there and see where it takes us, okay?"

"Where it takes us? To five percent sell-through,

that's where it takes us. For every female reader we gain, we'll lose two men. I guarantee it."

"No. Your stories are great, Beck, *this* story is great, that won't change. You're not going to lose men over a love interest for Mack. Most men have actually been in love, you know."

"But this is fantasy. They read my books to escape all that."

"To escape being in love?"

Beck closed his eyes. "That came out wrong."

Or maybe not. Weren't most men wanting to escape now and then from the female-directed rules of "relationship" into something nice and tidy like good guys blowing up bad guys?

Relationships had to be examined and worked on in exhaustive detail. Men had to be told they weren't doing this, that or the other to female satisfaction. And always the question, what happened to the wonderful romantic men they used to be?

The wonderful romantic men they used to be disappeared about the same time the adoring sweet women they were dating became critical, judgmental shrews.

"Just try it, Beck. Try it. Soften up the sex scenes. Especially make Tamara's self-pleasuring scene more real. Try that one first. And when Mack joins her, make him feel it in his heart as well as his dick."

"Alex—" Beck sighed. It was hopeless. When your editor and agent were against you, things were tough. Add in the members of the marketing department and the ever-dreaded focus groups, and you might as well bend over and take it.

If he had a dime for every person envious of a writer's so-called complete freedom in his work…

Well, if he did, he'd be rich enough to keep Mack's mind on his dick during a sex scene, where it belonged.

"Okay." He ran his hand over his aching head and jaw. "Just on the one scene with Tamara. See how it feels. How it reads."

"Wonderful. You're fabulous. It's going to be so much better, you'll be amazed, I promise."

"Right." He shook his head and hung up the phone harder than he needed to. Got to his feet and strode over to the window, pulling back the sheer curtains to gaze out at Madison Avenue.

Damn it to hell. He might have known this would hit eventually. This or something like it. He didn't know a single writer who hadn't come up against a brick wall at some point in his or her career. And Beck's journey so far had been relatively easy. Alex had picked him up when he was still unpublished, working as an editor, still learning the craft in his own writing and from that of his authors. She'd seen enough raw talent to judge him a good commercial risk.

After extensive revisions, his first book had sold, then his second and his third. Mackenzie "Mack" Adams had starred in six books in the past six years, and for a while it seemed Beck's star would never stop rising. Three years ago he'd quit his job to write full-time. Then the flattening sales, the apparent loss of reader interest.

And now back to extensive revisions. And the girlification of a true man's man.

Worse, to rewrite the scene the way Alex et al wanted him to, Beck was going to have to find a woman who would be willing to describe her masturbation practices for him.

Of all the research he'd done, this was potentially

both the most enjoyable and the most agonizing. Not to sound arrogant, but the women he'd dated hadn't needed to touch themselves when he was around. And asking old girlfriends their current autostimulation techniques wasn't the most tactful way to get back in touch.

No way would he ever admit to male friends he needed a woman to ask. He didn't have any female friends close enough to broach a topic like this. His brothers would tease him unmercifully or slug him if he suggested asking their significant others.

The ideal would be a sexually open complete stranger he could talk to and never see again. Like *that* was going to happen. Though if it were possible, HUSH was as likely a spot as any to find one.

This was all too depressing. Next he'd start contemplating hiring a hooker.

His cell rang again and he rolled his eyes and reached for it to check the display. He didn't feel like talking to anyone at the moment.

Oh.

Mom.

"Hi, Mom." He rubbed his forehead, waiting for his headache to get worse. He loved his mother, loved his whole family, but his idea of how much time was appropriate for a man his age to spend with them differed vastly from theirs.

"Hello, Beck, how's the writing going?"

"Fine. Just fine." She asked every call, to be polite, and every call he answered fine. His entire family was in the restaurant business, an Italian place on West 55th Street—he was the black sheep. They wouldn't care or understand about his line of work, so he generally didn't bother sharing.

And he was pretty sure asking his mother about masturbation would not be a good way to start.

"Thursday night is the thirtieth birthday party for your brother Jeffrey."

"I know." He screwed his eyes shut, the predicted worsening of his headache making its first throbbing appearance. Of course he knew, Dad had called him two days ago to remind him and Mom a week before that. "I'd really like to come. But I have revisions due on Friday, and it's going to be close."

"Sure, close, you can't get away for an hour?"

No use. He could try to explain that it wasn't just the minutes he'd spend away from his keyboard he'd miss. It was the mental buildup, the interruption, the wind-down time it would take to get back into his work. And how was he to know if Thursday night was going to be a particularly creative time, when everything would come together in a huge burst of output?

"I'll come if I can, Mom. I promise."

"Good enough. Everything okay there? You want me to send you some food to the hotel? Something decent? Some of your dad's osso bucco?"

"Thanks, Mom, they're feeding me fine."

"Okay. Okay. I'll go. But everyone wants to see you, the whole family misses you. You sit in that room all day long working, it's not healthy."

He chuckled. "I should be out in the fresh air?"

"I get it." She laughed. "You're not a little boy anymore. Moms are all the same. But if you need anything, you call me."

"I will."

"Even if you don't. Just to say hi. Okay?"

"Deal. Thanks for checking on me."

"You're a good man, Beck. I worry about you."

"I'm really fine. Bye, Mom." Beck clicked the phone off before she could start listing single women she knew, then stood there imagining her bustling to the front of the restaurant, making sure everything was perfect, flowers and candles on the tables, menus clean and carefully piled, staff in place, complimentary antipasto dishes lined up in a neat row.

That world could have been his.

Sometimes he thought he'd been switched at birth, and somewhere some serious scholarly couple were wondering how they had ended up with a boisterous half-Italian chef for a son.

He needed a drink.

More than that, he needed one out among people. Usually he was content to be in his room, or prowling the hotel; he was a loner at heart like most writers, something his jovial family of extroverts couldn't understand. Tonight, for some reason—probably that the soul was about to be ripped out of his life's work—he'd rather indulge his demons with strangers around than tackle them on his own.

And who knew? Maybe his sexually open female stranger was at the bar right now, waiting for him.

2

Note on Exhibit A waitstaff board:

Don't bend over near guy with mustache and cowboy hat who's at Exhibit A every night. He's an octopus; hands everywhere.
Jessie

IT TOOK ten strides to go from the window to the door of room 1457. May only took a few minutes to clue into that fact. And eight to go from the wall with the desk, to the wall next to the bed.

May had also clued into the fact that men who flew her halfway across the country and then backed out at the last minute with a lame-sounding excuse and then didn't call again really pissed her off.

May had tried ringing Trevor, but his voice mail had picked up. She'd left a message in a broken, pathetic, scared voice, asking him to call her. Which he hadn't. And that was over three hours ago.

Then she'd hated herself so much for sounding broken, pathetic and scared, she'd gotten pissed instead. Royally. Because what the hell was she supposed to do now?

Oh, sure, he'd been a total doll in the voice-mail message. He felt soooo bad about this unexpected and unavoidable—and she noticed, unspecified—schedule change. May was welcome to stay the full week on his dime. Enjoy the luxuries and amenities of the hotel to their fullest.

Yeah? Well considering she'd been planning to have sex all week, a spa, indoor pool and rooftop garden were not quite adequate substitutes. Neither were the plastic penises she'd discovered in a drawer, which might be anatomically correct, but had the distinct disadvantage of not being attached to sexy and fun-to-talk-to men.

Creeping home with her *tail* between her legs, instead of delicious and slightly sore memories, didn't sound remotely appealing. But then neither did staying here completely on her own in this overwhelming city, at a hotel populated by other people having all the naughty fun she was supposed to be having.

Not that sex had been the entire point, of course. Part of her had probably secretly hoped she and Trevor would hit it off emotionally, too. And maybe that was where part of her anger was coming from now—from the disappointment that it couldn't happen, and she was back to mourning Dan. But even if she and Trevor hadn't fallen for each other in any serious way, they would have had fun, and a week's adventure she'd always remember fondly.

Damn, but her toast was good and burned.

She whirled and headed for the phone, called Midwest Airlines and winced at the cost of changing her ticket. Jotted down the flight times on the hotel notepad under the childish caricature she'd done of Trevor as Satan. Couldn't be helped. She could go home standby on a flight tomorrow; the agent seemed to think the planes wouldn't be full.

Maybe that was best. She didn't belong here. With Trevor around, she could have managed it. On her own, it would just be too depressing.

Her cell phone rang and she hauled it out of her purse. Trevor?

Nope.

"Hi, Ginny."

"Hey, girlfriend. I can't believe you answered the phone! Why aren't you puffing and panting? I was just going to leave you a dirty voice mail."

May sank onto the bed, mortified to feel tears coming up. "Trevor's not coming."

"Hmm. Did you go down on him? I read in *Cosmo* that men who have—"

"*No,* not that kind of coming. I'm serious." The tears went back down and she smiled. "He's not coming to the hotel. At all. This entire week."

Ginny's gasp made her feel better. Her friend would understand. She'd tell May to rush back to Wisconsin and come over to her apartment, and they'd make sundaes together and rent a romantic movie and have a total girl—

"How are we going to find you someone else?"

May's jaw dropped. "Someone who?"

"Another guy for the week."

"Oh, right. You want me to advertise?"

"No, no. Walk into a fancy bar and smile at someone, that's probably all it takes. It's New York! You could probably go out and get Jerry Seinfeld or one of those guys from *Friends*."

"Ginny, this isn't a joke."

"I'm pretty sure Alec Baldwin still lives there. You might—"

"I was thinking of coming home."

"What?"

"I. Was. Thinking. Of—"

"Is it the money? I know the hotel is megabucks, but maybe you could spring for a couple of nights at least? Or move to another hotel?"

"Actually…" May gestured around the room and let her hand slap down on her thigh. "Trevor said he'd pay for me to stay at Hush even though he's not going to be here."

"What? And you're thinking about coming *home?* To *Oshkosh!"*

May sighed. She'd *thought* Ginny would understand. "What am I going to do here alone for a week?"

A thud came over the line. May winced. Her overly dramatic friend had dropped the phone and probably crumpled to the floor to make her point.

And okay, Ginny did have one. May sounded disgustingly whiny. And mousy. And naive. This was an amazing opportunity.

It just felt all wrong.

Ginny came back on the line and May placated her with promises to think it over, then dejectedly ended the call.

Fine. This totally sucked. She needed a drink. Granted, it was barely four o'clock, but who cared.

She flipped open the elegant leather-bound service menu, then paused.

Ginny had scored one point. Did May really want to come all the way to New York and only see the inside of an airport, a cab and a hotel room?

She wasn't brave enough to go hang out in a local bar, but the hotel bar would probably be okay. The very thing that made HUSH perfect for her and Trevor would make her feel safer, albeit conspicuous. The clientele at a hotel like this had to be all couples. Why else pay these prices? There were other hotels in New York just as luxurious for the single traveler. What made HUSH special was the emphasis on the erotic, and the assurance of tasteful discretion. Which meant couples. Unless someone was into some seriously expensive self-stimulation.

So yes, a few eyebrows might rise at the sight of a woman alone. But most likely not. The staff was undoubtedly trained not to raise eyebrows at anything. And the couples—honeymooners, marrieds trying to spice up their lives, about-to-pop-the-question daters—would be so into each other they'd barely give May a glance. Besides, she'd be channeling Veronica Lake big-time and give off movie star, off-limits vibes.

Done.

A wry smile curved her lips. So it wasn't quite the adventure she wanted. But it was still better than being home alone in her apartment with another frozen dinner, missing Dan.

Good.

She took off the city- and travel-smelling suit, refilled the tub, grown chilly in the hours she'd spent angsting, took a long, luxurious, fabulously scented whirlpool bath, helped herself to the lotions and felt much better. She unzipped her suitcase and, sighing, pulled out what was *supposed* to be the first outfit Trevor would take off her.

A black spaghetti-strap tank with built-in bra to show off her NFBs, aka "no fair boobs"—a nickname Ginny made up in high school, furious nature bestowed on May a slender body *and* full breasts.

Over that, a sheer gauzy top with red flowers. Next, she dragged on sheer black stockings, then a midthigh black skirt, and slipped her feet into spiky black heels that made her nearly six feet tall.

Never, ever, ever would she be caught dead in anything like this in Oshkosh. Not because people would be shocked by the outfit. Because they'd be shocked by *her* in the outfit.

She strode defiantly to the mirror, got her first look since she'd worn the clothes in the dressing room and bit her lip.

Actually, *she* was shocked by her in the outfit.

But New Yorkers wouldn't be. And people at HUSH wouldn't be. And she had nothing much more conservative to wear except the suit she'd brought for the plane, and she was *not* going to wear that tonight.

She'd wring some tiny drop of adventure out of this trip or die trying.

So.

Lipstick, subtle eyeshadow, darker blush than the apple-cheek pink she usually wore. She'd paid for a makeup lesson at her salon and had been pleased with the results, though frankly she didn't think she looked very much like herself. More like Veronica.

Onward, upward, clothes and makeup done, now for the attitude.

She smacked her lipsticky lips together, then pouted them out slightly and made her expression blank, cool, haughty.

Oh, that was good. Very good. This girl didn't come from Oshkosh. No way. This was a sophisticated woman of mystery, no doubt hiding depths of passion men would long to dive into. This was a woman who knew which men she wanted to dive and how to get them to do so. This woman could hold her own at the Erotique bar at HUSH Hotel in Manhattan, New York, U.S.A.

And that's exactly what this woman was going to do.

At the lobby entrance to the Erotique Bar at HUSH Hotel in Manhattan, New York, U.S.A., May/Veronica wavered. It was one thing to imagine herself striding confidently into a strange bar, another actually to do it.

She stood just inside the leaded glass doors and pretended to survey the room coolly, trying to control the panic launching her heart into triple time. A circular bar to the left, with pink lighting overhead, around it funky high black chairs with inverted triangle backs. To the right, tables on black carpet, with low round-backed leather armchairs in the same seafoam-green color as the lobby. Several empty seats at the bar, quite a few tables free. Where would she be least conspicuous?

Possibly at a table, but then if an unattached male did happen to be prowling around, she'd be stuck. Better to sit at the bar, tended by an attractive young woman who looked even taller than May, with ash-blond hair in a perfect French braid, the kind May would love to have instead of her long schoolgirl mop. Either that or the bravery to cut it all off.

She pulled out one of the fabulous chairs, which she coveted for her kitchen in a more neutral color, and sat. There. She'd done it. Maybe a curious glance or two from the couple on her right, but nothing more than that.

"Hello there." The bartender approached with an easy grin and a Southern accent. "How are you this evening?"

"Fine. Thanks." May couldn't help returning the woman's grin, even if it wasn't very Veronica-like of her, and instantly felt herself starting to relax.

"What can I get for you?"

Ulp. She supposed Miller Lite would not cut it here.

Or a blender drink with a cute umbrella. Okay. On to new adventures. "A…martini. Please."

The bartender gave a slight nod and waited expectantly. May tried not to panic. What else was she supposed to say? Shaken not stirred? A martini was a martini, no? Her father had always ordered them that way. Or not?

The bartender reached under the bar and slipped a one-page menu in front of her, heavy white paper, black bordered with an embossed pink HUSH logo at the top. "Just FYI, if you want something other than a straight gin or vodka martini, we have a specialty menu here. The sour apple and Cosmopolitans are our biggest sellers."

May nodded, grateful for the quick and gracious rescue and scanned the menu, trying not to bug her eyes out at the prices. She could have dinner at Ted's Diner in Oshkosh for the price of one drink here. But if Trevor was paying? "I'll have a Cosmopolitan."

"Coming right up." The bartender grinned again and moved off to start making the drink, holding the bottles up high when she poured, measuring off the doses with graceful flourishes. "Is this your first visit to Hush Hotel?"

"My first to New York, actually."

"Where are you from?"

May picked up a black box of HUSH emblazoned matches. How much did she want to tell? "Wisconsin originally."

"I'm from Oklahoma. Came to seek my fortune in the Big Apple as a makeup artist." She set the deep pink drink down in front of May. "You try that and tell me what you think."

May took a sip and smiled. Icy cold, fruity and sweet, but not too, very nice. "Really good."

"Thought you might like it."

"You want to be a makeup artist? Like in salons?"

"No, no." The bartender laughed. "Movies, video, TV, stage, fashion. Anywhere I can get."

May gritted her teeth under a closed-lips smile. *Like in salons?* She better just keep her mouth shut. Every time she opened it, fresh farm manure came spilling out. "What got you into that?"

The bartender shrugged her black-uniform clad shoulders. "I guess I love the idea of transforming a person into something or someone he or she isn't."

"I can imagine." May fingered the black and pink coaster under her drink. Yeah, she and Veronica could imagine all too well the appeal of that concept.

"Good evening, Miss."

"Good evening, sir. How are you this evening?" The bartender's voice greeting the new arrival changed to a quieter, more respectful tone. Even her accent lessened. But May could swear that under the quiet respect, she could detect amusement. Amusement which also danced in the bartender's dark blue eyes.

May glanced over, overcome by curiosity, and registered a man, she'd guess midthirties, tall, nicely built, clean-cut, jacket no tie, about to sit two chairs to her left. She turned back to her Cosmopolitan, wanting to gawk and see if he was really as good-looking as he appeared at first glance, but fearful of broadcasting her wide-eyed interest. Who would a man like that be meeting? Probably Catherine Zeta-Jones's twin. Funny he hadn't chosen one of the quiet, cozy tables.

Or was he on his own, too? And wouldn't Ginny love that?

"I'm quite pissed off, Shandi. And you?"

She laughed. "Doing great as always, Beck, what'll you have?"

"Martini, you know how I like them."

"I do." She grinned and reached for a beautiful blue bottle of gin. "Bombay blue sapphire, into which vermouth is barely introduced, shake well and drop in a twist."

"Perfect."

May watched her—Shandi—make his drink with fluid movements, precise and practiced, and wondered what had pissed the man off and whether Shandi would ask him. Maybe his date had stood him up, too. And wouldn't that be...interesting.

She felt his eyes on her and kept her gaze determinedly ahead, the chance of relaxation quickly melting into a fresh attack of nerves. Maybe she should finish her drink and get back downstairs, to—

What? Sit miserably in her room contemplating her return trip tomorrow and her navel?

Too depressing. But she wished he'd either speak to her or stop staring. Maybe she needed to goad him into doing one or the other.

She turned to him with back-off coldness in her eyes and immediately wished she hadn't. His were an unusual blue color, hard to pinpoint in the relatively dim light of the bar. But their effect on May was not remotely hard to determine. From his perspective, her cold wintry stare was probably experiencing a nice spring thaw. She yanked her eyes back to her drink and took a big sip, wishing for a Miller Lite she could chug and be done with.

"How's that drink?"

She took the time for a slow breath, then couldn't

help herself; she threw him another glance. Yes, ten seconds later he was still incredibly attractive. "Very good."

Okay, she got three syllables out, that was fabulous. Now it was up to her, the freeze-off or the invitation for more chatter? A vision made the decision for her: of the big, empty, made-for-sex room with her in it, alone, watching the same TV shows she could watch in Oshkosh. "How's your martini?"

When he didn't answer right away, she turned to look at him again. He was half smiling, only one side of his mouth turned up, as if she amused him, but not entirely. His gaze had turned speculative. Was he wondering why she was alone?

"Excellent." He lifted his glass toward her. "I'm Beck."

"I'm…" She considered giving a fake name, then couldn't think of one besides Veronica, and what if he turned out to be someone she really liked? Then she'd have to explain a fake name and it would all be way too complicated to extract herself from a lie like that, because—

"May." She said her name slowly, at the same time telling her whirling brain to calm the hell down.

"Are you meeting someone, May?"

Oh, now there was a question. "I was."

"But now you're not?"

She shook her head, congratulating herself for not saying too much.

"Hmm." He lifted his glass to his mouth, but didn't drink right away. "I suppose I should say I'm sorry to hear that."

"But you're not?"

He smiled with both sides of his mouth this time and took the delayed sip. "No."

May's heart started a race she was pretty sure it

couldn't win without killing her. She instructed her face and body to remain expressionless and motionless. As if she were posing for the cover of *People* magazine, and movement would make her look blurry.

Beck stood with his drink, and instead of moving into the chair next to her as she expected, came up right behind her. "Would you like to move to a table where we can talk?"

She turned and looked into his eyes again, bracing herself for the shock of attraction so she wouldn't react visibly this time. He was gorgeous, even this close with every possible flaw exposed—except she couldn't find any. Square jaw, faint grooves down the sides of his cheeks, ridged nose with great personality, killer blue-gray eyes with black lashes, full masculine mouth, cool wheat-colored slightly spiky hair…all her Serious Hunk requirements were met and then some.

But beyond that, an air of easy confidence that made Dan and Trevor and the other men she knew look apologetic in comparison. And an intensity under his relaxed in-control aura, as if an incredible brain was hard at work noticing and assessing everything and everyone around him.

She wanted to put her tongue out and pant like a puppy.

At the same time—if things had worked out as planned, she'd be rolling in the very expensive hay with Trevor right now. Yes, he'd dumped her, yes, he hadn't called back to see if she was okay, but it felt a little uncomfortable to be chatting up a total stranger. To be this *excited* by a total stranger.

Or was that just too spinelessly overloyal of her?

Trevor wasn't here. Nor would he be. And some instinct told her work had nothing to do with why. Plus, if he'd encouraged her to stay the week on his dime without him—well he had to know in a place like this something might happen. It wasn't as if she'd be doing anything but talking to Beck tonight. She wasn't even sure how much loyalty she did owe Trevor, since nothing had ever been quantified vis-à-vis their relationsh—

"Yes? No?"

"I'm sorry." She resisted the urge to thwack herself on the head. Beck wanted a simple answer to a simple question, while she sat here analyzing every possible pro and con as if she were contemplating a major life change. "That would be nice."

There. Decision. How about that?

They moved to a table for four near the window, facing what she thought was East 41st Street, but she wasn't swell on directions, so it could be Madison Avenue, taking their drinks with them. May sat in one of the round-backed low leather chairs and was taken aback when instead of taking a seat across from her, Beck sank into the chair next to her, with quite a bit of athletic grace, she might add, extended his long legs under the table and leaned back, hands folded across his abdomen, looking as if he was settling in for a long evening.

May tucked her own legs back under her chair and took a healthy swallow of her Cosmopolitan, hoping she looked like an experienced drinker and not someone desperate to chase off nerves. Never mind the few sips she had were already affecting her.

"So, May. What happened to Prince Charming?"

"Prince who?"

"Whoever you were supposed to meet." He adjusted his chair so his assessing stare hit her directly and made her have to work harder not to appear flustered. "Don't tell me he got invited to another…ball?"

His emphasis on the word "ball" made May swallow her next sip quickly so she didn't spit it out. Okay, that seemed rude as hell to her, but maybe in New York and at HUSH hotel, it was acceptable to talk to strangers about their sex lives. She'd keep her ice-coating thick and play along. "Some matter in the running of the kingdom unavoidably detained him."

Beck's brief grin delighted her. "Will His Majesty show up at a later time?"

She helped herself to cashews from the green pedestal bowl that looked like a giant martini glass. If she said no, she'd effectively be admitting her availability.

"No." Another casual sip of her drink, and she was starting to feel quite happy and brave and warm all over, thankyouverymuch.

"Was this a serious boyfriend? A fiancé? A husband?"

May's jaw clenched, then released. She couldn't lie. She was a terrible liar. And the truth fit her Veronica image so much better. "A man I met recently."

She felt like cheering. Oh, that came out soooo well, just tossed off casually as if she did this all the time. Fun! This was so fun!

"I see."

She was sure he did; he brightened like a lightbulb in fact. And now must be making all kinds of sordid assumptions about her. Which May was amused to find delighted her. She'd be gone tomorrow, what did she care what he thought? "I was supposed to stay the week. Now I'm leaving in the morning."

"Fleeing before the clock strikes midnight and leaves you in rags surrounded by rodents, lizards and a pumpkin."

She barely contained a smile. "Something like that."

"Where's home?"

"Where's yours?"

"Right here in Manhattan." He gave no sign her refusal to answer his question bothered or surprised him. "Fifty-six blocks north and one west."

She opened her mouth to ask what he was doing in a hotel this expensive if he lived close by, but then it hit her she had no idea if he was staying here, or if he regularly patrolled the bar looking for women with rooms whose dates hadn't showed up. "I see."

"I've written a book set here at Hush." He winked, which did something stupidly fluttery to her insides. "Free publicity for them equals free room for me."

"Nice deal."

"It is." His next glance made her feel she was supposed to react somehow. Beck…books…something *was* nagging at her brain. What was it?

"So…what is your book about?"

"A serial killer in a hotel."

"Ah." She toasted him. "Charming."

"Thank you." He grinned and clinked her glass with his.

Serial killer. Beck. Books… Her father was always reading some grisly shoot-'em-up book or other that drove May's mother crazy. Wasn't one of his favorite authors…

"Beck Desmond?"

He nodded, watching her carefully. "That's me."

She managed a cool nod while her insides experienced tornadic activity. Holy moly. She, Little Miss Nobody From Nowhere, was sitting at a swanky hotel in one of the world's most important cities chatting with a mega-celebrity of the publishing world. Ginny would die. "My father reads your books."

"Oh, nice." He seemed genuinely pleased, which surprised her. "I take it you don't."

She shook her head. "I tried one, but we didn't work out."

He looked at her intently with those killer blue eyes, then back at his drink, as if he were considering whether to ask her something…maybe something personal? Or was she dreaming? Her heart started pounding. She had a dangerous feeling that "yes" would be an all-too easy reaction.

"Can I ask why you didn't like my book? For professional reasons, not because you wounded my ego."

May reached for her glass to buy time and hide her disappointment that he'd asked the wrong type of question. How the heck was she supposed to handle this one? "They're not my thing."

"How so?"

She threw him a look and he held up his hand. "I don't mean to push, but it's actually relevant right now. I'd really like to know."

"Okay." She tried not to fidget; Veronica would never fidget. And May had a degree in English; she knew perfectly well why she didn't like his books. But how the hell did you say things like "flat characterization" to a multipublished successful author? "This is just personal. And totally subjective."

"Keeping that in mind, I'm interested in your opinion."

"Why mine?"

"Because, May, you're a woman."

Maybe he didn't mean to make that sound like he wanted to see her naked, but for some reason that's how it sounded. Most likely alcohol had affected her hearing, and her fantasies about him had affected her brain and HUSH hotel had affected her hormones and the combination had made her insane.

"Yes." She gave the perfect Veronica pause. "I am a woman."

"And I need a woman's opinion."

"Okay." She'd hoped for a sexier answer. "Well, for one thing, your books are pretty grisly."

"Granted. What's the other thing?"

"What other thing?"

"You said 'for one thing.' Which made me think there had to be others."

She took a deep breath, wondering if he'd fling his drink in her face and stalk out of the bar if she told the truth. "I like books that are more character-driven. Yours are plot-driven. It's just a question of taste."

He frowned, then leaned forward so suddenly, she nearly jumped back. Except this close to him she could see the shadow of stubble darkening the grooves in his cheeks, see a stray hair escaping from his otherwise neat short sideburns, get a close-up view of his very sexy mouth, and the urge to jump back left very, very quickly. "What would you think if I had the hero fall in love?"

Her eyes shot from his mouth to his eyes. "*Mack? Fall in love?*"

He nodded. "This is what my agent and editor want me to do. They think more people—specifically more women—would read the books if Mack had a girlfriend or a…puppy."

She couldn't help smiling. He said puppy the way most people would say sexually transmitted disease. "I take it you don't agree."

"It would ruin him. But not as much of this is up to me as most people think, so I'm stuck trying it."

"You think falling in love ruins people."

He laughed and showed a dimple that surprised her. "Often. But in this case, I'm just concerned with Mack."

"A kinder, gentler, butt-kicking assassin detective."

"Exactly." He gave her a significant glance and looked around, as if afraid of being overheard, though there was no one close enough. "And they want more emotion in the sex scenes."

"Hmm." She had no idea what to say to that. She wasn't a writer, but sex with Dan had always been emotional, and she couldn't imagine trying to portray it any other way. Maybe if she'd gotten the chance with Trevor she would have discovered what unemotional sex was like…but even there, she'd hoped something more would come of it.

"Plus…" Beck drained his drink and put it back exactly in the center of the napkin, looking slightly uncomfortable for the first time since she'd met him. A man and woman seated themselves at the next table and Beck motioned May closer. She leaned in and caught a whiff of how a very sexy celebrity writer smelled: like expensive male sin.

"It's sexual, do you mind?"

Oh, my God, oh, my God. "Not at all."

"It won't shock you?"

"Nothing shocks me." May nearly bit her tongue. What a line! Nothing shocks her! She was cruising on such a—

God, please don't let her look shocked.

"Good." He grimaced and rubbed his hand back and forth over his chin.

Uh-oh. May took a sip of her drink to try and keep calm.

"I have to find a woman who will tell me how she pleasures herself."

Alcohol hit the back of her throat at the same time she gasped, and there was no escaping the humiliation of choking in front of Beck Desmond, who probably talked about masturbation every day with all his New York friends, along with politics, the Yankee/Mets scores and what they planned to order for lunch. Luckily she could blame her blush on her near-death experience.

But damn, damn, *damn.* Served her right for acting as if she could handle anything.

A glass of water appeared on the table next to her and she smiled gratefully at Shandi, still unable to speak.

"Is he behaving himself?" Shandi sent a mock-stern look over to Beck; May managed a nod and gulped water which soothed her throat considerably.

Beck gave an exaggerated shrug of innocence. "Is making people choke to death considered misbehaving?"

"It comes close." Shandi discreetly slid a book next to him, one of his. "Can you sign this for Janice Foster, our general manager?"

"Sure." He took a pen out of his jacket pocket. "She reads my books?"

"Her brother does. Sign to Jack Foster, please."

Beck sent May a look of exasperation that made her grin, signed the book and handed it back to Shandi, who returned to the bar to serve new customers.

"Maybe your agent and editor have a point."

"Apparently I have to find out." Beck leaned forward and touched her bare arm. "I'm sorry if I shocked you."

She waved away his concern. "That wasn't shock, that was swallowing wrong."

"So may I ask you something fairly personal?"

"How I pleasure myself?" She could have cheered. The line came out smoothly and she wasn't even blushing. Perhaps Cosmopolitans should become part of her and Veronica's nightly routine.

"Um…yes." *He* looked embarrassed. Ha!

She let her left eyebrow arch. "You'd call that a *fairly* personal question?"

"Actually, I call it research."

"I barely know you."

"Then I'll tell you whatever you want to know."

"How do *you* pleasure yourself?"

He laughed, a loud long laugh that made the couple next to them glance over, and made May swell with a peculiar giddy joy. Ginny would be sooo proud of her. Hell, *she* was proud of her.

"Touché. But it was worth a shot. It seemed like fate that you were here alone when I needed a woman to ask. Otherwise I'd risk getting socked in the nose by an angry date."

"I really didn't mind." But she really *did* hope he'd drop it. No way could she discuss something like that and hope to remain Veronica. She'd never even talked about that with Dan.

"Do you *have* to go home tomorrow?"

She finished the last of her drink and set it down, sensing she needed to wind the evening up before she got herself in any more trouble. "Why?"

"I think you can guess."

"You want to soften me up so I'll tell you my sexual secrets?"

He held out both hands in an innocently helpless gesture. "It's my job."

She laughed. "Now there's a line."

"Believe me, I suffer for my art." His eyes narrowed in a sexy grin which faded and left her that blue-gray intense gaze that made her want to promise him her first-born child. "Even just writing something down and shoving it under my door before you leave would help. I'm in Room 1217."

She stood and tilted her head, so Veronica could survey him coolly. "I'll think about it."

"Thanks." He held out his hand. "I hope if staying the week is a possibility you'll consider it. It would be nice to have someone to talk to."

"About sex."

"About everything. But yes, that. You could be a valuable resource for this new direction they want me to take, May. My consultant on the female perspective, if you will."

She shook his hand, then left hers lying in his, neither of them making a move to pull away. "I'll think about that, too."

"Good. Sleep well." He winked and waggled his eyebrows. "And if you get lonely in the middle of the night and want to talk dirty, give me a call."

She arched an I-don't-*think*-so eyebrow and swept out of the bar, leaving his laughter behind, her head spinning with possibilities. Of course she couldn't stay the week now, but oh, my God, she wanted more of how she'd been and what she'd felt with him tonight.

No way could her Veronica act last a week. Sooner or later she'd betray who she really was and he'd think she was a complete fool. Tonight had been perfect—a perfect fantasy. Pursue the farce any longer, and she'd ruin it, not only going forward, but also retroactively.

She crossed the lobby, where the cat she'd seen earlier followed her flight with condemning green eyes, as if May was a total disgrace to femininity. Down the hall, into the elevator, up to her floor, into her room, and the first thing she did was grab a black and pink HUSH pen, tear off the silly sketch of Trevor-Satan, and on the thick hotel notepaper, write "Beck Desmond, 1217."

Just in case she forgot.

3

Note on Luxe spa board:

Trevor's latest babe-ola here today for the full spa treatment. Don't forget Brazilian wax instead of bikini. And low-sodium lunch so she doesn't "puff."
Marta
(Rolling eyes)

AT TWO O'CLOCK the next afternoon, May emerged—not from the airport in Milwaukee—from the HUSH spa, Luxe. Okay, so she hadn't quite gotten on the eleven-thirty plane. But the way she was feeling right now, Veronica Lake et al should be looking to emulate *her*. What an experience. Hot stone massage, luxury warm glove manicure, pedicure, caviar extract and seaweed protein facial, waxing, gourmet lunch, haircut and makeover….

She was buffed, polished, soothed, relaxed, well-fed—the entire series of appointments had been glorious, beginning to end, with the merest exception of the waxing. Apparently Brazilian wax was not a special kind of wax, *ahem*. Obviously not a single hip New York woman ever committed the horrible faux pas of having more than a tiny strip of pubic hair at the base of her pelvis.

None. Anywhere else. *Nada. Niente.* Not even…
back there.

Ouch.

Other than that, it had been ecstasy. She'd even gotten up her nerve to cut her hair chin-length for the first
time, after Nico, the stylist, practically threatened her
life if she refused. And he was right—she loved it. *Loved*
it. A blunt bob with bangs that fell just above her newly
made-up eyes, which made her look mysterious and
peekaboo sexy. She felt as beautiful and cool and sophisticated as she'd pretended to be last night. She
wished Trevor could see her like this. For that matter,
she wanted to go knock on Beck Desmond's door to
show him the new look. Hell, fax Dan a photo and make
it a four-way.

She'd woken up this morning in the bed she should
have been sharing with Trevor, with her brain full of
Beck Desmond and regret that her adventure at HUSH
had been so limited. She'd intended to pack and leave
for the airport, but discovered the fabulous invitation
with the schedule for her own private spa day slipped
under her door. Didn't take long for her to decide she'd
be nuts to pass up the opportunity.

The invitation must have originated with Trevor.
What a sweetheart. He must have worried, thinking how
lonely and lost she'd be feeling and called the hotel to
arrange the pampering for her morning. And here she'd
been so upset that he made no effort to get in touch with
her after he cancelled. He probably hadn't wanted to
spoil the surprise.

So she'd take the five-thirty plane home. At least she
could say she'd really had an adventure now. At least
she had something to show for her trip. No, she hadn't

had a week of wild sex with a charming handsome man, but Dan I'm-bored-of-you Thompson couldn't say she was dull and predictable now. At least not to look at.

She sailed into her room, changed into her sensible traveling suit with only a brief burst of longing for all the new clothes she wouldn't get a chance to wear this week, and packed up her things, stopping every now and then to glance in the mirror. Great hair, perfect nails, soft lovely feet, newly cleaned-up brows… Who was this fabulous woman? A tiny wistful thought flew into her head that this fabulous woman would be sort of wasted back home in now-dateless Oshkosh.

Packing done, she glanced at the clock. About an hour before she had to leave. Why spend it sitting here?

She wandered out into the hall, carrying her sketch pad, not sure where her feet would take her, thinking that if she had control of the universe, fate would intervene and put Beck Desmond in her path, and at least give her a reason to take the seven-thirty flight….

But of course fate never did what she thought it was supposed to do.

Her feet took her down the hall into the elevator, where she saw Roof Garden on the label next to the top button. Perfect. She rode all the way up, smiling languidly at a man—not Beck, sigh—who glanced away from his date more than once to check her out. If this kept up, by the time she tried to leave, she'd be so full of herself she probably wouldn't fit through the door.

Alone in the elevator for the climb to the rooftop, she emerged and wandered out into an extraordinarily beautiful and elaborate garden. The space had been cleverly segmented with columns and railings and pergolas, giving the illusion of a series of rooms. Nasturtiums and morning glories cascaded from metal railings, clematis and grapevines climbed white trellises. An espaliered fruit tree here, juniper and white pine there, pots and pots of hanging greenery and flowers everywhere else. A bower with a swing. A rose garden with a statue fountain, a partly enclosed space with a rock garden sprinkled with exquisite bonsai—May could happily spend her whole week here with a good book or two.

Except it seemed bizarre to have a slice of nature on a roof in the middle of one of the world's biggest cities. A glance up, and the unrelenting geometric aggression of the surrounding buildings made her feel uncomfortable, isolated and alone. She took out a charcoal pencil tucked in a pocket of her sketch pad, and drew angular jagged lines and weary hopeless greenery, a satire of a garden choked off from the grassy meadows and trees that should cradle it.

Sketch done, she closed the pad, a little relieved, as if some of the poison had been allowed out of her system, and wandered over to where an elderly woman in blue slacks knelt on a black cushion tending an herb garden, humming and occasionally singing snippets of some song in a high lovely voice.

"Good morning." The woman broke off her hum and greeted May as if they were friends—her eyes warm, intelligent and bright blue in her lined face—then went on snipping sprigs of rosemary, placing them into an open wicker basket at her side. "Lovely day."

"Oh. Yes." May glanced around in surprise, wondering why she hadn't registered that it was. Maybe because beautiful days to her meant peaceful woodlands and fields and sunshine-smelling breezes, not skyscrapers and smog and distant traffic noise. The temperature was cooler than the previous day; a light wind pushed puffy clouds past overhead. There were still buildings everywhere, hemming her in, but the roof of HUSH was high enough that she could at least see over some of the others and not feel victim to their oppression. "The garden is beautiful."

"Thank you." The woman removed a flowered cotton glove and held out her perfectly manicured hand, making May pleased that her own nails were up to snuff. "I'm Clarissa Armstrong."

"May Ellison." She shook Clarissa's strong soft hand and found herself smiling genuinely. The older woman was beautiful—she must have been absolutely stunning in her day. Her linen blouse, sprigged with tiny blue and purple irises, green leaves and dots of yellow, was freshly pressed and immaculate. May would bet that even though Clarissa worked in and around dirt all day, none of it was allowed to stick to her.

"The garden isn't only beautiful. We grow herbs and vegetables for the restaurant here. And the plants keep the temperature of the roof down, which saves the hotel money on cooling."

"I didn't know that." May sank down and inhaled sage and thyme. "Oh, these remind me of Mom's garden at home."

"Where's home?"

"Wisconsin." She grinned wryly. No point pretending anymore that she was anyone but herself. "Oshkosh."

"Ah, a lovely state." Clarissa glanced at May, then clipped a few stems of basil. "Have you visited New York before?"

"No."

"What do you think?" The question came out quickly,

as if she had some reason other than politeness for wanting to know.

"It's…very different. A little…overwhelming. But the hotel is wonderful."

"Indeed."

A flash of black and pink leaped out of the garden and materialized from behind Clarissa—the cat May had seen in the lobby. It stood, head tipped slightly, studying May as if considering her future worth.

Clarissa chuckled. "There you are, Eartha."

"Eartha?"

"Eartha Kitty." Clarissa smiled mischievously. "The official hotel cat. She has the run of the place. Showed up one day and never left. I have a catnip patch for her up here and she loves to chase insects."

May crouched and extended a hand to the beautiful animal, speaking soothingly. The cat sat, curled her tail around herself and gave May a stare that would shame an empress. Next time May needed lessons in cool, she'd have to remember that look.

"So, have you visited the bar, Erotique?"

May shot Clarissa a sharp glance, but to all appearances, she was still concentrating on basil. "I was there last night."

"Really?" Her voice was a little too casual. "Lovely isn't it. And Shandi makes a fabulous Cosmopolitan."

"How did you know I—" Her cell phone rang and she stood, pulling it out of her purse. "Excuse me. Hello?"

"Hey gorgeous, how was your appointment this morning?"

"Trevor!" May let out the cry of pleasure, then for some reason thought of her newly nude privates which

Trevor wouldn't get to see, and blushed. Then immediately had to banish an enticing image of Beck watching her touch herself the way she looked now. "Why aren't you here?"

"I would be if I could, baby. Work is nuts, I can't even begin to tell you how much I'd rather be there with you."

"Me, too." She smiled into the phone and tried not to think how much she hated being called "baby." Her fault for not saying something at the beginning of their friendship.

"So what's your plan for this afternoon?"

She sighed. "I'm going home."

"What?"

"I can't let you spend this kind of money, Trevor. Not if you're not here to enjoy it with me."

She noticed the woman glancing curiously at her and turned away, tossing her head to move strands of hair the wind blew into her mouth.

"Are you sure?"

"Yes." She frowned. She didn't sound that sure. A man's tall athletic form caught her eye through a trellis and her heartbeat sped before she registered it wasn't Beck and turned back toward Clarissa.

"Whatever you want. But I owe you the week, so if you decide to stay it's fine. We can still reschedule another time soon. Just think about it."

"Thanks, Trevor."

"Hey, you're entirely welcome. I just wish—" A woman's voice sounded in the background. "I gotta go, babe, my appointment's here. I'll call you later."

"Oh. Okay. I'll—" The phone clicked off in her ear and left May standing with her mouth forming more words that didn't get to come out.

Obviously an important appointment.

Clarissa gave her another glance. May lifted her head to the breeze, thinking of the vast green tree-lined farmlands of her childhood and wondering philosophically how any child could thrive in this claustrophobic concrete wasteland, where gardens existed on roofs and in boxes as some kind of antidote to their surroundings, instead of an extension of them.

Because if she stood here wondering these things—philosophically of course—she wouldn't have to wonder why something didn't seem quite right about Trevor Little and this whole situation.

"How did you happen to come to New York?"

May looked sharply down at Clarissa, who'd moved closer to dig peacefully around some thyme, as if she hadn't just been obviously eavesdropping and as if she thought it was her perfect right to ask personal questions. Eartha had disappeared, or she probably would have demanded a few details, too. May wanted to say "none of your business" but she wasn't raised to be able to say that to people.

"To meet a friend here."

"Trevor Little?"

May's mouth dropped open. She was sure she hadn't mentioned more than Trevor's first name. "How do you know him?"

Clarissa serenely brushed a fly off her cheek and went back to the thyme. "Most of the staff at the hotel know Mr. Little."

May froze with the phone halfway back into her purse. A cloud swept over the sun, in an absurdly melodramatic accompaniment to Clarissa's statement.

"He…has some business dealings with the hotel?" Maybe? Please? With the cherry on top?

The pitying look Clarissa sent her was expected. "Trevor Little is often a guest here at Hush."

The tiny bite of acid in her otherwise gentle tone told May everything she needed to know. Charming Trevor was a regular here with women, probably a different one every time, maybe sometimes two at once, perhaps an occasional animal, as well. That shouldn't surprise her. Or shock her. Or disappoint her.

But of course it was doing all three. *Damn.*

So, okay, regroup. Just because this was a once-in-a-lifetime event for her didn't mean it had to be for him. He brought women here all the time? Big deal. Not like he promised May romance forever. Not like she'd forgotten to bring a box of condoms to avoid catching anything icky.

"Did you enjoy your spa visit this morning?" Snips of thyme went into the basket and Clarissa moved gracefully on to the sage.

"How did you know about that?"

"Tuesday morning is always the spa appointment."

May took a step toward her, her brain struggling against more unpleasant thoughts. Tuesday…always the spa appointment? For every woman he brought here? Trevor hadn't called this morning and booked it especially for her?

God she was gullible. "The flowers yesterday?"

"I always arrange them myself."

May nodded miserably. "Two dozen red roses on Mondays."

"Lovely, aren't they. Jewelry tomorrow and I think lingerie Thursday, then chocolate on Friday."

May's elegant spa luncheon threatened to turn inelegant on her. She wanted to run to the airport, fly home and dive into a half gallon of Häagen-Dazs Vanilla Swiss Almond, then get miracle-grow cream for her pubic hair to come back as fast as possible, so she could put this entire fiasco behind her. Maybe Dan was right, but dull and predictable had to be better than this.

Clarissa rocked back on her heels, then slowly up to standing, knees still bent as if they wouldn't straighten quickly. "Oof. I'm getting too old for this job."

"Let me get that." May darted forward to lift the basket so Clarissa wouldn't have to bend again.

"Thank you, dear." Clarissa put a warm hand on May's arm, and May caught a whiff of a light floral perfume amid the strong herbal scents from the basket. "I don't want you to think I'm a gossip. I told you because you shouldn't hesitate to spend as much of his money as possible. He has plenty and then some. Stay the week and have yourself a ball. It's a lovely hotel, the city is peerless."

May stooped to get the shears still on the edge of the herbal bed and held them out. "I don't think I can do that."

"Of course you can." Clarissa tucked the shears into her basket and slung it over her arm. "I met a man in Paris, in 1958, when I was studying at the Sorbonne. Jean-Jacques. We arranged to meet for a week in a hotel on Corsica and he never showed. I met another man at the hotel, a Mr. Wisely, a new widower, a wonderful and very special lover. We had a splendid week together, and I sent all the bills to Jean-Jacques."

"He paid?"

"Of course. He owed me." She winked and May could well imagine how men had flocked around her—and probably still did. "Turned out Jean-Jacques had a wife who had other plans for him that week. That happens, you know. *Quite* frequently."

She gave May a significant look, and the lightbulb finally went on in May's naive too-trusting brain. Of course. The last little bit of fantasy excitement for the planned week crumbled like the dirt of the garden. "Trevor is married."

Clarissa put a comforting hand on her shoulder. "Most of Trevor's...*friends* knew and didn't mind. But I had a feeling you didn't and would."

"Yes." A classic understatement. "Thank you."

"You're welcome. I've been very indiscreet, the hotel management would be furious with me. But we women must stick together."

May smiled and took a step back, wondering how to say politely that she needed to get the heck out of here because she had to hit something.

"Go. Go ahead, I understand." Clarissa made a shooing motion with her free hand. "You'll feel better when you've had a good cry or whatever you need to do. Then pick yourself up and have the time of your life. It's waiting for you here this week, don't waste it."

"Thank you."

"And come see me anytime, dear." Her eyes warmed and crinkled into a smile. "I take care of all the plants in the hotel, so if you need a friendly face or someone to talk to, just ask anyone and they'll find me."

May nodded and fled the garden, down the elevator, into her room where she flung herself on the bed. Oh, this was so special. She wanted to call Trevor and scream at him, call his wife and let her know what a jerk her husband was.

Except it wasn't up to May to bust up a marriage, however twisted. Maybe his wife was just as bad. Maybe they got adjoining rooms at HUSH that had peepholes bored between them for their mutual viewing pleasure.

What the hell was she going to do now? Part of her would love to stay the week as Clarissa had suggested, making sure Trevor paid, literally, for his sin against her. But wouldn't that make May just as sleazy? Bring her down to his slug-trail level?

Call her Pollyanna, but she needed a better reason to stay.

She sat up in disgust and caught a glimpse of her transformed self in the mirror opposite the bed—her sexy haircut, her wide anxious eyes, the flattering blush of anger. What would Veronica do? Veronica would be on the phone to Beck Desmond saying she was entirely available for whatever he had in mind. And then some.

Her head dropped onto her fists and she groaned in frustration. But she wasn't Veronica, not really. She was Pollyanna Ellison, lacking the confidence to stay, not quite willing to leave….

She got off the bed and paced the room until she realized what her body really needed was a good workout. She'd go to the hotel pool and swim off her frustration. Maybe an answer would come to her. Maybe some sign would smack her between the eyes and make the entire situation clear.

With any luck, fate would step in on cue for once, and the sign would look a whole lot like Beck Desmond.

Note pinned to the staff board:

Beck Desmond and Trevor's castaway spotted cocktailing at Erotique last night.
Pass it on.
Anonymous

BECK GLANCED at the clock on his laptop and rolled his eyes. Just shoot him now. A whole morning blown and now half the afternoon. May hadn't called; she'd probably gone back to wherever home was, and he'd wasted time hoping she'd lend him the magic he needed to get his career back on track. While he waited, he'd tried to be productive by thinking about what kind of woman his hero Mack would fall in love with. One who could sustain Mack *and* Beck's interest over what Beck desperately hoped would be the springboard to several more books.

First he'd tried imagining a petite sweet blonde who could smooth over Mack's rough edges, soften him with her own softness. But who the hell could write about sweetness for four hundred pages without turning diabetic? He'd done a character sketch for Ms. Sugar-Pie, character interview, backstory, background, and nearly fallen asleep.

No way.

Then he'd tried the other tack. A tall, brunette, tough-talking, kick-ass woman who could equal Mack in the lethal department. Her character and backstory were fascinating—at least to him. But he wasn't sure female readers, who were the whole damn reason he had to do this, would like her.

So where did that leave him? Back where he started

after he hung up with his agent yesterday afternoon—hanging off a precipice by his fingernails. Alex wanted the revisions completed by the end of the damn week. If his take on this new direction they wanted, featuring a kinder, gentler Mack, wasn't approved, or if readers didn't buy it, then this contract could be his last. And his parents and brothers, who regarded his success like a too-fancy car he couldn't afford and shouldn't be driving, would be able to mouth told-you-sos behind his back.

He shoved away from the desk and pitched the latest empty water bottle into the black and chrome wastebasket, stood and grabbed his key card. He had to get out of here. A turn around the hotel would probably do him some good. Maybe he'd see a woman who would fit the bill, make that magical something click in his brain. Maybe he'd get lucky and find out that May was still here, though last night she'd seemed pretty determined to leave.

Why he'd pinned so much hope on May, he wasn't exactly sure. It had seemed so provident last night when he was in need of a single, sexually liberated woman that he found her the minute he walked into Erotique. She seemed to take everything in stride, seemed to be the perfect sophisticated done-it-all type he was after. And it didn't hurt that she was beautiful and damned appealing—he'd be the first to admit his determination to follow up with her was heightened by attraction. But he was asking a lot, maybe too much too soon. Maybe he'd misjudged her, and she wasn't as worldly as she appeared—or as he was so anxious she be. All a moot point if she was gone.

He strode out into the hall, and took the elevator to the hotel library, where the first murder in his story took place, and where Mack met Tamara, the woman of his fantasies, who now might have to become Susie, the woman of his dreams.

Just not his wettest ones.

The location could spark ideas about this Susie character—or whatever he named her—to make her fascinating and complex enough to interest him *and* his readers *and* Mack. And maybe he could bump into one of the more chatty members of the staff who would spill whether May was still in the hotel. If such a miracle occurred, this time he could ease into the request for help a little more suavely than nice-to-meet-you-how-do-you-masturbate?

Yeah, right. Grasping at straws was such an intelligent and constructive way to proceed. Especially if the one he grasped was the last for the poor camel of his career. The damn frustrating thing about creativity was that it couldn't be forced, either into existence or to fit where it wasn't natural. Maybe it made him too much of a "guy," but this soften-Mack-up, make-him-fall-in-love thing was feeling like a suit handed down from a five-hundred pound man that everyone expected Beck to make flattering.

He stalked through the double glass doors, into the large room, not a dark, leathery, men's-club library, but airy and plant-filled and light. Comfortable cream-colored armchairs and sofas loaded with colored pillows sat randomly in singles, pairs and triples, each equipped with adjustable reading lamps and small padded footstools alongside. The richly polished bookcases, in a sleek two-tone wood design, held classics, reference books and a large collection of tasteful erotica.

Beck scanned the room and immediately struck gold. Watering one of the ficus near the floor-to-ceiling windows, the grande dame of HUSH, Clarissa Armstrong. He'd met her his first day here, nearly three months ago, and they'd hit it off right away, having in common a love of old movies, fine wines and human nature. Whatever was going on in the hotel, she knew about it and was willing to tell, though loyalty and discretion prevented her from spilling anything damaging. If May was still here, Clarissa would know.

"Good afternoon, Clarissa."

"Beck, hello, wonderful to see you as always." She smiled her gracious, beautiful smile, and turned off the water. "What can I do for you?"

"Not a thing." He tried to smile nonchalantly, knowing if he launched immediately into the real reason he wanted to talk to her, he and May would be HUSH's next hot-gossip item. "You look lovely today as usual."

Clarissa rolled her eyes, blushing at his compliment. "Save it for your younger fans. This old woman has been around too long for you to bother with. What's on your mind?"

He chuckled and freed the hose from the corner of the wooden planter where it had snagged. "Beautiful day."

She sent him a sharp look of amusement that told him she was willing to play along with the small-talk thing, but only for so long. "Yes, isn't it. What are you up to?"

"Just taking a walk, see if any new ideas jump at me."

"Aha." She smiled and rolled the hose neatly back onto its cylinder. "And have they?"

"Not really." He pushed his hands into his pockets and rocked back on his heels like a nervous kid. *For God's sake, Beck, just ask her.* "Any interesting newcomers to the hotel?"

Clarissa's delicate gray eyebrows arched; under them

her eyes danced. "Would you by any chance be interested in hearing tales of a lady from Wisconsin with whom you shared a cozy drink last night?"

He had to hold his mouth closed in order not to look as astonished as he felt. So much for avoiding being the topic of gossip. "I might be."

"I thought as much."

He rolled his eyes and grinned at her. "Okay, what can you tell me?"

"Not that I condone spreading gossip you understand, but I believe this certain lady from Wisconsin might be open to a new escort this week if she can be convinced to stay, since hers…failed to materialize."

Her disdain made Beck narrow his eyes. "You know him?"

"He is well known at Hush, yes."

"Let me guess…rich married playboy, brings women here while he's supposedly on business trips…"

Clarissa plucked a yellowing leaf off the ficus and peered up into the topmost branches, looking for more. "I said nothing of the kind."

He nodded. She didn't need to. Which did two things. One, it made him want to punch the guy's lights out for being a sleazebag, and two, it confirmed his initial feeling that May was the perfect person to help him with this first scene Alex wanted revised. Why a tiny part of him was disappointed to be proven right on this point, he was not anxious to investigate.

Whether May had enough depth to help him with female input into the rest of the revisions remained to be seen. Falling in love might not be Beck's strong suit, but it didn't generally get dealt to women like May, either. Anyone who would accept the kind of relationship she'd planned for this week had seen and done it all—but would probably feel next to nothing either seeing it or doing it.

None of which had any bearing on his immediate need, which was to find May and make sure she planned to stay at least a little longer.

"How determined is she to leave?"

Clarissa grabbed the wooden box planter and turned it with surprising strength, so the other side of the tree faced the light. "I believe she could be convinced to stay."

Beck grinned. "With the right kind of persuasion?"

"Naughty boy." She gave him a dazzling smile. "I don't suppose you are interested in knowing where she is right now?"

"Gee." He gave a pretend nonchalant shrug. "I might be."

She winked and leaned close. "Not that I'm prone to snooping you understand."

"Of course not."

"I believe Ms. May Ellison was last seen heading for the hotel pool."

Beck shook his head. "Now how could you possibly know that?"

"Pure chance, my dear. Happenstance. Coincidence." Clarissa narrowed her eyes mysteriously and gave him a light tap on the shoulder. "And in this case, I think maybe fate."

Beck laughed uneasily. She was at it already. In a few hours, the staff of HUSH would start laying bets on him and May getting together. Little did they know his interest in her was purely—well, *primarily*—professional.

He blew a kiss to Clarissa, thanked her again, and

strode back out of the library, heading for his room and his swim trunks. In any case, he knew where to find May; she hadn't checked out yet, and he had another shot at convincing her to help him. He might not be a millionaire playboy, but he wasn't an ex-con felon, either. Everyone wanted something, everyone could be bought.

He just needed to figure out what May Ellison's price was, and pay it.

4

ROUGHLY TWO MILLISECONDS after Beck entered the pool room, clutching the fresh warm towel the men's changing room attendant had handed him, he spotted May—though the room was nearly empty, so it wasn't exactly a significant accomplishment. She sported a new flattering haircut, and a very plain turquoise one-piece bathing suit—not what he thought he'd see. The new haircut, sure, but on her body he'd expected a three hundred dollar microbikini, made not to touch water, but to be admired on a salon-tanned body lounging in a poolside chaise. To his eyes, the simple design of the suit, the way it followed and flattered the very graceful, very female lines of her tall figure made it sexier than the skimpiest G-string.

Even though he was after her for professional reasons, at the moment his thoughts were taking a fairly unprofessional turn.

But then he'd always preferred women modestly clothed—relatively modestly, he was hardly a Puritan—whose sexuality simmered below the surface and erupted in a volcanic surprise behind closed doors. Women who advertised to all who cared to gawk did little for him. What did they leave for the fun of discovery?

May hadn't seen him; she seemed distracted, or

tense; a small frown bunched her mouth and eyebrows. She walked to the edge of the water without looking around, bent and dove smoothly in, surfacing to attack the length of the pool with strong, clean strokes at a pace he probably couldn't keep up for more than half a lap.

At the end of ten, she executed another flawless turn and kept going.

Again, unexpected. Not a surprise that she was physically fit; she probably had a personal trainer to keep her assets in shape for whatever millionaire she was entertaining that week. But the no-nonsense athletic determination to dominate the pool—that, he wouldn't have expected from the languid beauty he'd chatted with last night.

Or the lack of hesitation to get newly styled hair wet and chlorinated.

He tossed his towel onto one of the white chairs grouped around tables on the room's periphery and sat on another, content for now to watch her swim. This room was one of his favorites in the hotel. Mack had discovered a body floating here, a sensational place for a ghoulish midnight drowning.

The pool was a long, narrow rectangle in the center of the tiled gray floor, open to natural light below a glass ceiling with wooden beams that looked like the spine and ribs of an enormous geometric animal. At night, chrome sconces at wide intervals shot bright white up the walls, leaving stripes of dark in between, while underwater lights lit the pool brilliant blue in a room that at that hour looked otherwise like a black-and-white movie. On a raised platform at one end, a Jacuzzi frothed and bubbled, currently occupied by a couple blissfully unaware that anyone or anything else existed but them.

Envy jabbed him until he remembered his last time in a Jacuzzi, with his former girlfriend, Mary Ann, who'd gotten tipsy and furious that he was paying more attention to his nearly due manuscript than to her, and why couldn't he ever forget about that writing stuff and be with her like they used to be?

He never knew how to answer that question, another of the many loaded ones the opposite sex hurled so effortlessly. It seemed pointless to ask why she couldn't stop yelling at him for the career that had excited her in the first place. Did she think the books wrote themselves? That armies of elves did the work while he had hours to lounge in a Jacuzzi and tell her she was gorgeous? Didn't it occur to her that during the beginning of their relationship he was between books and had more time?

Lap fifteen and May swam on, maybe slowing a bit.

Or was Beck just not a good person in a relationship, as he'd been told more than once, usually by a ballistic soon-to-be-ex girlfriend? The women he hooked up with he enjoyed, no question. Unfortunately, there always seemed to be a huge gap between how they expected him to behave and how he was inclined to. He never could seem to ascribe the level of importance to being attached they seemed to think was necessary. Not only was he apparently insufficiently involved in anticipating and satisfying their needs, but he constantly failed to notice things he was supposed to notice, and failed to say things they thought beyond obvious he should say…

Lap twenty, May changed from crawl to breaststroke, downshifting her workout.

At the same time, Beck wasn't the type for short flings based merely on attraction like so many of his gender. He preferred women in his bed to be those he wanted around for a lot longer than a night or two or five. Obviously May Ellison was cut from a different cloth on that issue.

Lap twenty-five, she gentled her breaststroke to a lazy glide forward, water building and breaking leisurely over her nose. Finally, she hoisted herself easily out of the pool and walked to the table with her towel on it, not noticing him or showing any interest in her surroundings.

If he wanted to talk to her, this was his chance.

Uncharacteristically nervous, he got up and sauntered over to where she stood, her back to him, pressing the towel to her face, water making her suit and body gleam.

"May."

She jumped and turned, wrapping the towel hurriedly around her waist in a show of modesty that seemed out of character. "You startled me."

"Sorry." He found a grin on his face where he hadn't planned one, aware his pleasure at seeing her had too much to do with his gender. And hers. And the theoretical potential of a physical combination thereof. Not nearly enough to do with his book.

The turquoise of her suit was right for her skin, not too bright, not too dull, and lit her eyes so their color glowed from her face. The deep scooped neckline and wide-placed straps emphasized the graceful line of her collarbone and the enticing depth of her cleavage. Hair smoothed back by her swim, a surprising blush coloring her makeup-free face, she looked nothing like a sophisticated mistress and everything like a Midwestern farm girl. Which, in his opinion, made her ten times more alluring.

The book, Beck. This is about the book. "Had a good swim?"

"Yes, wonderful."

"You look like a pro."

"Oh." She glanced toward the pool, then took a deep breath. "Swim team."

"High school or college?"

"Both."

He nodded. College-educated. Which ruled out a high school dropout getting by in life on her back. Interesting. "So have you decided to stay at Hush?"

"I don't—" She lifted her chin. "Yes."

"How long?"

She glanced to the side yet again. "Probably the week."

He gritted his teeth, the elation she was staying short-lived. She was distracted. Or unwilling to talk to him. Or both. Maybe he'd turned her off last night with his request, though she hadn't seemed bothered at the time. Maybe she thought he was coming on to her and now that she'd decided to stay, she was trying to freeze him off. Maybe she already had another billionaire lined up after the last one jilted her, and she no longer needed to waste time talking to Beck.

All understandable. But the fact remained that he needed help on his book and she was—

Her slight gasp made him follow her gaze.

The pool was empty; the two other swimmers had left the room. Blue water undulated quietly, reflecting the light pouring through the glass ceiling in wobbly patterns interrupted by shadows of the thick wooden beams.

Beyond the pool, maybe ten yards away from where they stood, he saw what she'd been glancing at, and what had made her gasp. The couple in the Jacuzzi had just stopped kissing. Not leisurely romantic kissing, but serious I-want-you-now-and-I-intend-to-have-you kissing. The woman, a dark beautiful brunette, was raised up in her lover's arms, and by the look of concentration on his face, they were attempting to make it happen right there, right then.

"Oh, my God." May whispered the words beside him, though he couldn't tell whether in anticipation or horror.

The woman gave a low moan and closed her eyes. She began to move slowly up and down, an expression of rapture on her face. The dark man glanced toward May and Beck, then away, apparently unperturbed—or maybe thrilled—they were watching. He slowly reached up to untie the woman's halter suit, then brought it down so her full breasts were exposed, aureoles large, nipples dark.

Beck drew in a long breath, becoming aroused, as much by being trapped with May in the intimacy of what they were seeing as by the show itself.

The man cupped his lover's beautiful breasts, thumbing the nipples. She tipped her head back, full red lips parted blissfully. A soft female moan reached them; her up and down movements became faster.

Beside Beck, May gasped again, made an involuntary movement. Was she about to leave? His instinct begged her to stay. Without her, the exhibitionism would seem empty, sleazy; he'd be embarrassed to be watching alone. With her beside him, the couple provided a tantalizing erotic interlude.

She stayed. The woman moaned again; she was supermodel-gorgeous, sensual. Beck observed her objectively, his senses focused more on May than the woman's movie-star perfection.

Her lover pushed her breasts up into two lush handfuls, then bent and took the tip of one into his mouth. She cried out, clutched his head; her up-and-down movements grew wilder.

May's breath went out, rushed back in. Was she shocked or aroused? He couldn't tell, didn't want to look to find out in case he embarrassed her or intruded on her thrill.

One of the man's hands disappeared under the water, then the other. He lifted the woman suddenly, water streaming off them both, then turned and knelt, sitting his lover on the edge of the tub, her long legs spread wide.

Beck took a small step back, trying to catch May in his peripheral vision, wanting to see her face, but afraid he'd shatter the freeze-frame moment, afraid he'd push something she didn't want pushed if they acknowledged each other. He sensed her tension, saw her rock-stillness, but couldn't tell if she was horny or horrified.

The man started his thrusting rhythm again, buttocks bunching and relaxing; the woman propped herself on her hands, arms straight behind her, hair swinging as she arched back.

Beck turned to May, uninterested in seeing any more of the now totally public show. "May?"

She turned toward him immediately as if she, too, was relieved to look away. "Yes?"

Her eyes were bright, lips full, cheeks flushed, breath high—she was massively turned on. That fact shot his own arousal higher than it had been watching the live sex act.

The woman's moans increased; she panted, moaned again, building to a long cry, which the man inside her echoed shortly after, in a deeper, harsher vocalization.

Beck waited tensely. May would look back now; she'd want to see porn-flick Romeo's orgasmic bliss.

She didn't. She kept her clear blue eyes on his, and the chemistry between them leaped to life as if someone had thrown a match into a puddle of gasoline.

His cock responded first and his brain soon after, caught in the sensual power of May Ellison's eyes. How many other men had been trapped there? He wanted to peel her suit from her body, lift her onto the table beside them, see her skin living and rosy against the white painted wood, immerse himself hard in her slender tight body and take them both where the other couple had just been.

"My room or yours?" The words came out low and urgent and as soon as he heard them from his own mouth he wanted them back.

May blinked and blinked again, as if she was startled out of a delicious dream. "What?"

He closed his eyes briefly. What was he thinking? He wasn't. At least not with his brain. "Nothing. Never mind. Just…got the wrong signal."

"Oh. I…I'm sorry. I didn't mean—"

"My mistake."

"No. No, it was fine. I'm just not. I don't…" She lifted her hand, then let it drop helplessly, and gestured to the ladies' changing room entrance. "I should go."

He opened his mouth to stop her, then stopped himself instead. This encounter had gone from good to bad to worse, until she was dying to get away from him. Though for all he knew, she just wanted to get back to her new date to share the story of what she'd seen here so they could come back and reenact it.

Frustration hit him. "You'll be around?"

"Yes." She was already backing away from him. His

frustration turned to a strange panic, like in grade school when he'd wanted to ask Mindy Jacobs out, had been talking to her outside the lunchroom, minutes ticking by with no asking happening, just pressure strangling his vocal cords until her giggling friends had come to her rescue.

"May."

"Yes." She stopped edging away.

"Are you going to be alone here this week?"

She glanced at the couple enjoying their afterglow back in the Jacuzzi, then turned to Beck, eyes calm and direct, a slight tip of her head making her look the sensual siren again. "Yes. I am."

"Can I call you?"

"To help with your book?"

He put a hand to the back of his neck. The book. God, he hadn't even been thinking of it. For once. "And because we're both here alone and company is nice."

The woman in the Jacuzzi burst out laughing and Beck cringed. Yeah, Mindy didn't think he was that smooth in high school, either.

May shot an angry glare over to the tub, then relaxed. He turned to find the couple still immersed in each other, and smiled at his and May's shared paranoia, and her willingness to defend him. "What do you say?"

"I'd like that." She sent him a sexy smile; at the same time a blush stained her cheeks. Then she turned and walked unselfconsciously through the door to the ladies' changing area.

Beck stared after her, hands on his hips, fascinated more than he cared to be, more than two brief meetings warranted, though as a writer it was his job to be fascinated by people. Plenty of women sent deliberate go and stop signals, enjoying the power it gave them, but what kind of woman sent them with what appeared to be utter sincerity on both counts?

Whatever kind it was, the more he saw of May Ellison, the more interested he was in finding out.

MAY REACHED her room and noticed another invitation under her door. Oh, great. What other wild spontaneous thing had Trevor planned months in advance for every woman he brought here?

This one turned out to be a reservation for dinner that night at Amuse Bouche, the hotel's elegant restaurant. Oh, what a lovely publicly lonely meal that would be. At eight o'clock—she'd starve to death long before that.

She spread her arms out wide and let herself fall back onto the king-size bed in what had narrowly escaped being her and Trevor's room. Staring at the spotless ceiling, she thought about how the sprinkler head looked like the spur on a cowboy's boot. And how the air in the room smelled fresh, and slightly herbal, like the lobby. And how the rooms were fabulously insulated—she could barely hear the traffic noises and wasn't aware by so much as a thud that anyone else was staying on her floor. And finally, yes, how she couldn't believe she'd just stood in a public area and watched people having sex.

She screwed her eyes tight shut, heat gathering in her cheeks and forehead. How she'd managed to maintain anything resembling cool she had no idea. On the one hand, she'd been mortified. And shocked. And vaguely repelled. And...well, Geez-o-Pete as her father always said, they were having *sex* in *public*.

On the other hand...

She rolled over and lay on her stomach, hands in fists

close to her hips, head turned toward the window. As mortified and shocked and vaguely repelled as she'd been, she'd also been as wildly and completely and urgently turned-on as she'd ever been in her life.

Not only because the couple was young and extremely attractive. Not only because the excitement they took in each other expanded to include Beck and her. But also, because standing there watching these two beautiful people pleasure each other, she'd felt such a strong pull to Beck, such a strangely intimate erotic bond, it was almost as if they'd been having sex themselves. Except they hadn't and that was her fault.

The squawking call of a seagull pulled her off the bed and drew her to the window. She pushed back the curtain and watched the bird swoop by, then away on some mysterious errand.

It was easy to forget Manhattan was an island. Right now she felt like one herself. A deserted island, in the middle of an ocean of strangeness. She couldn't even call and report something like this to Ginny. For all Ginny's breezy fascination with life in the fast lane, she was, at heart, the daughter her minister father raised.

For a few minutes spent watching the bustling street below, May indulged in a longing for Dan, for her quiet, controlled, all-planned-out life in Oshkosh. Working at the university nine-to-five, five days a week. Working out at the university pool. Coming home, eating with Dan or out with Ginny or alone. Sometimes catching a movie. Sleeping alone or with Dan. It was a nice routine. Comforting. Fulfilling, for all but a few strange restless moments now and then.

Nothing like coming to New York, being jilted, then deciding to stay anyway, Trevor be damned. Getting the makeover of her life. Watching strangers have sex in public. Being propositioned by a fabulous celebrity author.

And how did she react to her first shot at this big thrill she thought she was after? She'd tossed Beck a few panicked sentence fragments and fled back here to the dull safety of her room as fast as her waxed legs would carry her.

Oh, yeah. She totally belonged in the fast lane. You just couldn't rattle old May, no way, no how. Unless you did something out-of-control wild, like breathed in her presence.

She let the curtain fall, blocking out the sight of the city, grabbed her pad and sketched a picture of herself, drowning in the buildings of New York, as if they were quicksand.

He'd wanted her. Which was exactly what she hoped for. What she'd decided to stay for while she was swimming. But when faced with what she hoped for and decided to stay for…she freaked.

Maybe she should just—

May dropped the sketch pad, put her fists to the sides of her face and growled in frustration and disgust. If she thought "maybe she should just go home" one more time, she was going to scream. Maybe she this, maybe she that… Maybe she'd been named May, short for Maybe.

Yes. Yes, she was staying. *No.* No, she wasn't going home.

Yes, she'd been caught in a bizarre situation, which… uh…life in Oshkosh hadn't quite prepared her for. *No,* she couldn't imagine anything short of growing up in a swinger's club would prepare one for public sex.

Yes, she was going to stay and have a good time if it

killed her. *No,* she was not going to allow herself to be
easily flustered again. Veronica Lake would be super-
glued to her image. No more cracks, no more flaws, no
more failures.

And *yes.* If Beck asked again if she'd like to go to
his room, she'd say *yes.* If he asked if she'd tell him how
she masturbated, she'd say yes. How she gave blow
jobs? *Yes.* How one day she did seventeen men at once
before breakfast? *Yes, yes, yes,* she was going to say yes
and not look back or second-, third- and fourth-guess
herself to death.

In fact she was going to call Beck right now and invite him to dinner with her that night. And in a page out
of Clarissa's no doubt fascinating book, she'd graciously allow Trevor to pay. Ha! She marched over to
the phone, dialed the first three numbers of Beck's extension and slammed the phone down. Smacked herself
on the head. Maybe—

No. More. Maybe. She was going to do this. Another way.

Over at the room's elegant desk, she yanked open a
drawer. Notecards with envelopes, the kind that held her
spa and dinner invitations. Perfect. She picked up the
black pen with the pink HUSH logo and sat in the cush-
ioned desk chair to write.

Dear Beck,
I'd like to invite you to dinner with me at the hotel
restaurant tonight. I've made a reservation at
eight. See you there.
May

Smiling she stuffed the note into the envelope, smiling wickedly. Nice touch not asking him to RSVP, just

telling him she'd be there and assuming he'd show. That should make up for some of her caught-off-guard ineptitude by the pool.

So. All that was behind her now. Onward and upward, Veronica. She'd pop out to Beck's room right now, and shove the note under the door....

No. She'd call the concierge and have the note delivered. Much classier. And then Beck wouldn't happen to hear her and fling open the door while she was still shoving the note under, and she wouldn't be caught squatting in the hall outside his room looking like a doofus. From now on, she'd do this right.

Because there was no longer any "maybe" involved. She was going to have her big thrill this week at HUSH Hotel with Beck Desmond, and not one blessed thing was going to stop her.

Especially not herself.

5

Note on Amuse Bouche Restaurant staff board:

I assume we're still serving Trevor's champagne to Ms. Ellison and whomever she's dining with tonight? I'll go ahead unless I hear otherwise.
Jean

SEVEN FIFTY-FIVE and time for Veronica. Wearing the little black dress she'd chosen for dinner with Beck, May studied herself in the full-length mirror on the bathroom door. She'd owned the dress for two years, but this was its first outing, and she adored it as much as the day she bought it. The dress had thin straps and a wide scooped neckline that flirted with the tops of her breasts—and she better stop thinking how empty the space between them looked without Dan's grandmother's locket. Below, the soft material hugged her body, not so tightly that she'd get those I-really-needed-a-larger-size horizontal creases across her abdomen, but tight enough. She'd worn a strapless bra, so if the straps maneuvered their way off one shoulder or the other… *Oops!* No problem. Quite the opposite.

She'd even managed to get her hair and makeup done nearly as well as Nico and his henchwomen earlier at Luxe.

Beck had called after receiving her invitation, and since May expected that he might, Veronica had been firmly in control. She'd pitched her voice low and borderline suggestive, managed some fabulous lilting laughs and even ended the call with a "see you tonight" that sounded as if she was hot and naked already.

This was going to be a great night. Dinner dates with men involved only a lot of nodding and beaming. How hard could it be? She was even ready for his questions about her solo sex life.

She was pretty sure.

But first…some things you needed a girlfriend for, and getting ready for a hot date was one of them.

She rushed to her purse and dug her cell phone out to call Ginny.

"Hello?"

"It's May."

"May! You better not be calling me from Oshkosh…"

"No, I'm still in New York."

Long loud sigh of relief. "Thank God. Now tell me everything."

"Well…for one, I got a makeover." She turned one way and then the other in front of the mirror, enjoying the heck out of her uncharacteristic vanity.

"Ohmigosh, a *good* makeover?"

May laughed. "Yes, an incredible one."

"Not like the free one we got from Huckaby's Salon where they fried your hair and turned mine orange and then made us up like Brides of Dracula?"

"Not like that."

"Tell me."

May went into elaborate detail, the massage, the hair, the nails, the skin, the lunch, the Brazilian…

"Ow!"

"Yeah, no kidding. That part wasn't the most fun I've ever had."

"I've read about them, but…" Ginny made a shuddering sound. "So what are you going to do tonight?"

"Funny you should ask…"

Ginny gasped. "You have a date! I knew you'd find someone. Who is he?"

"Beck Desmond."

"No way. *No way.* You are totally lying."

"I'm not." She laughed and turned away from the mirror. "I'm really not."

"My God, Beck Desmond is even cuter than Alec Baldwin. I saw his picture in *People.* How did this happen?"

"He's at the hotel writing a book."

"Shut up!" Ginny demanded the entire story, which May told her, minus the spectacle in the hot tub.

"Oh, oh, oh, I'm so excited, I'm probably more excited than *you.* Okay, so what are you wearing?"

"Remember that black dress we bought at Boston Store, two years ago?"

"Ohmigawd, he's going to get a stiffy just *looking* at you. I love that dress! The one Dan never let you wear."

May frowned. *Let* her wear? "He just never thought it was right. I mean how many fancy occasions did he take me to?"

"Um…let's see, that would be…none." Ginny's voice was sharp. She hadn't taken kindly to Dan skewering May's heart, which was her role as best friend, one May would gladly take on if the skewer had been in the other hand.

"In any case, it's perfect for my date tonight."

"I'll say. I'm so glad you didn't leave New York. I hope

it works out with Beck, even just for this week. You deserve someone who thinks you're as amazing as you are."

May rolled her eyes at the subtle dig. Even when she and Dan were dating, Ginny hadn't been his biggest fan. She meant well, and wanted May to be happy. She just didn't understand the degree to which Dan had been that happiness. "Thanks. I better go."

"Okay, but I will require a detailed postmortem."

"Done. See ya." She clicked off the phone, stuffed it back into her purse, grateful for Ginny's infectious enthusiasm. One last glance in the mirror and she was ready.

So. Onward.

Deep breath, hand on the doorknob, then door open, and out into the cool hallway, down the elevator, one foot elegantly placed in front of the other, hips swaying but not too much, all the way across the lobby, where Eartha Kitty sat on one of the black chairs all alone, bathing herself, pink gem-studded collar sparkling in the light. As May passed, Eartha interrupted her paw-washing activity to deliver a long green haughty stare.

May winked. "I hear you. We are queens of the world who need no one. I won't forget that tonight."

At the entrance to the restaurant on the far side of Erotique, the gorgeous—of course—black-haired maitre d' greeted her with a friendly-yet-professional smile that showed stunning white teeth against his dark-toned skin.

"Good evening and welcome to Amuse Bouche, Ms. Ellison."

"Good evening…" She trailed off, since she'd been about to give her name for the reservation, and gave him a demure smile instead.

"Your table is ready, would you like to sit or wait for your companion to arrive?"

Which was more polite? To heck with that, which was more alluring? If she waited here, Beck could see the full effect of her dress, which she hoped he found considerable. "I'll wait. I'm sure he won't be long."

"No he won't be." His voice was right behind her. "Hello, May."

She affected the perfect pose, the perfect parted lips, the perfect sensually nonchalant expression, turned, met his gaze, and broke into a wide goofy smile she couldn't stop. Something about looking into those eyes made her giddy.

But smiling was fine, even Veronica could smile, though May would prefer sultry. And guess what, he was smiling just as hard as she was, making the dimple indent his cheek. "Hello, Beck."

"You look stunning this evening."

"You're quite stunning yourself." No lie. He wore a light summer suit, a shirt with a hint of blue and a blue-gray abstract tie that brought out the same hues in those haunting eyes. Classy, cool, fresh and…unbearably sexy.

Steady, Veronica. You're in charge tonight.

They followed the maitre d' into the nearly full restaurant where couples and occasional foursomes sat at well-spaced tables similar to those in the bar next door. The atmosphere was casually elegant, and the discreet use of partitions created the illusion of intimacy at each table. Oh, wouldn't it be nice to get used to living like this. And happy day, they were seated at one of the cozy twosomes against the wall, separated from the tables behind and ahead by slender black urns holding dried arrangements of pink roses, pencil cattails and wheat, punctuated by dramatically gnarled lengths of thin black branches. No doubt Clarissa's artistry at work.

A waiter, tall, lean and gracious, showed up seconds after their pink napkins hit their laps, and introduced himself as George. Seconds later, unexpectedly, another waiter—no, he was probably the sommelier, known in her family as "the wine guy"— brought over a bottle of champagne and a silver ice bucket.

Oh, now that would hit the spot. Beck must have called in the order ahead. An auspicious beginning. May sent him a cool smile, trying not to look overly pleased, as if men ordered bottles of expensive champagne for her every day of the week.

Except instead of wearing a smug only-for-you-darling expression, he was looking blank.

The sommelier presented the bottle for approval. To May. Which he wouldn't if Beck had ordered it.

Oh, no. Champagne on Tuesday at dinner. Another item on the Trevor agenda.

She studied the label, not registering a single word, and nodded her who-the-hell-knows approval to the Wine Guy, who untwisted the bottle's wire cage, took the cork out with a soft pop and poured for both of them. Thank God she didn't have to go through the farce of tasting it. What she knew about wine would fit in a single-cell amoeba.

"Enjoy your dinner." Mr. Wine Guy smiled, nestled the bottle back into the ice bucket and left in search of his next duty.

May gestured to the bubble-filled crystal. "I hope you like champagne. I thought it would be a nice start to the evening."

"Very." Beck grinned, and his dimple tucked itself again in his right cheek, such a surprise in a lean masculine face, like a tiny part of his childhood hadn't wanted to let go. "Excellent choice, too."

Whew. Unless he was just being polite. "Are you a connoisseur?"

He shrugged modestly, which meant he probably knew everything ever written on the subject. "I like a good glass of wine."

"I hope you'll order some for dinner." And save her farm girl butt.

"Happy to." He accepted his menu from George, lifted his champagne flute and looked at her slyly over the top. "Here's to you staying the week."

"Thank you." She clinked her glass with his and lifted it to her mouth, keeping the eye contact going, not letting on how thrilling and unnerving it was not to look away. The champagne tickled past her lips, over her tongue and danced down her throat. Oh that was delicious. Too delicious. In her nervous state, she was going to have to work hard not to gulp it.

"And to your new haircut."

"Thank you." She clinked again and drank more, hoping he'd keep toasting until she had enough in her to relax.

"And to getting to know each other while you're here."

May did more clinking and took an extra long sip at that one, surprised she was already regretting how short the time would be. But for just a second it sounded as if he really did want to get to know her. Except of course, it was Veronica he wanted to know, really. And how to market his books to women. And how she…did that thing to herself.

Anyway, that would have to do.

She studied her menu, trying not to feel awkward

about the silence between them. The choices were fabulous, inventive, unusual. She wanted to come here
every night and try everything. Panko crumbs? Diver
scallops? Arugula? A far cry from bratwurst and fish fry.
Would Oshkosh be safety and relief or confinement and
boredom after such a week?

"Penny for them."

She jerked her eyes off the menu and up to his face,
wondering in a strange dislocated thought how his thick
short spiky hair would feel under her fingers. He wanted
to know what she was thinking…how could she tell
him? "I was thinking about home."

"Wanting to go back or glad you're not there or hoping you didn't leave the stove on?"

She laughed. "Mostly the second."

"Do you visit hotels like HUSH often?"

Gulp. She narrowed her eyes in sultry inspiration.
"What do you think?"

He tapped his finger on the side of his champagne
flute. "To be honest, I'm not sure."

"No?" Why wasn't he? Had she slipped somewhere?

"There's something about you that doesn't quite fit
the mold."

"Hmm." What the hell did he mean by that? Her Ivory
girl complexion? Sophistication positively not dripping
off of her? Faint odor of fertilizer? "How intriguing."

"It is."

She lifted her chin and met his eyes squarely.
"Good."

"What made you decide to stay?"

You. She should open her mouth and say it; she had
the perfect, perfect setup. "Oh…a lot of things."

Shit.

"Like?"

"You. For instance." Okay, that wasn't as good as if she'd come out with it the first time, but it was a close second.

"Really?"

She ran her finger around the rim of her glass, dipped it into the champagne and sucked the drops off her finger, not daring to look at him. "Mmm-hmm."

He mumbled something under his breath, and then she did dare look at him, a sex-goddess peek through her lashes. She got a very good eyeful of what Veronica could do to a man when she was at her best.

Not the best eyeful, granted, the table was in the way for that.

"I'm curious about something."

She kept the sudden alarm off her face. Of course he was going to ask about *that,* she knew he was, she was practically inviting it, so just go with the flow. "Yes?"

"What kind of kid were you?"

The question was so unexpected, she had no idea how to answer. What kind of kid grew up to be Veronica Lake? No way could she invent anything she could keep track of all week. Might as well tell the truth. "Shy. Quiet. A loner mostly."

"Siblings?"

Siblings? Not cup size, not favorite position, not how she touched herself, in lurid detail, please? "A brother and a sister, much older. They were out of the house by the time I was big enough to notice. Why?"

"Part of getting to know you."

"I wouldn't have thought that was important for what you needed from me."

"It's not."

She arched an eyebrow, letting it ask the question for her. *Then why do you want to know?*

George chose to appear at that extremely inopportune time. "Have you decided what you'd like to order?"

May's teeth clenched in a frustrated imitation of a smile. She wanted to hear what would have come out of Beck's mouth, not what he wanted to put in it. For a fantasy second she'd imagined him saying, *Because I want to know everything about you, you intrigue me as no woman ever has, marry me and have my babies immediately.*

Which—sigh—was such a May thing to want him to say. She was Veronica, here to have an adventure, to stay cool, aloof and uninvolved, like Eartha Kitty back in the lobby. To wow him with her womanhood. Not to immediately begin calculating the probability of long-term success in a relationship.

No wonder she had bored Dan.

In the meantime, George and Beck were still politely waiting for her to get the glazed look off her face and order.

"I'll have the shrimp tempura appetizer and the seared salmon salad." She folded her menu, caught herself hoping her choices were chic enough and instantly chided herself. Who cared? She was going to eat what she wanted to eat. Besides, the shrimp were battered in Japanese panko crumbs, whatever those were, and you couldn't tell her that wasn't chic.

George took Beck's order—salad and steak, so what was she so worried about?—poured them more champagne and left.

"What were *you* like as a kid?" She tipped her head to one side, letting her new hairdo swing out over her nearly bare shoulder. Much safer topic than why he was so curious about her.

"A lot like you. In a house with two athletic brothers, I was small, studious, introverted."

"Small?" She studied his broad shoulders as if she were contemplating her next meal.

A sexy half smile turned up the left corner of his mouth. "I grew."

"And did that change your image?"

"Girls noticed me, yes."

"I can just imagine."

"What about you, were boys tripping over themselves to serve you then, too?"

She succeeded in not looking startled at the idea of men tripping over themselves to serve her then *or* now, and drank champagne, feeling more like Veronica every second. "Not remotely."

"No?"

She opened her eyes wide and shook her head quickly, as if surprised he would dare question her.

"Interesting."

"Why?"

"Because you strike me as the kind of woman with plenty of experience handling men."

Ha! Oh, she could practically cry from happiness.

"Ahhh." She drew the syllable out, her international woman of mystery persona in full throttle. "Well, things changed."

"What happened?"

She set her glass down and straightened her shoulders so her breasts pushed forward. "I grew."

He chuckled; his eyes flicked down and back up. "And did that change your image?"

"Men noticed me, yes."

"I can imagine."

She held his smile, watched his eyes warm, then darken, making sure none of the shock she felt at how strongly she was attracted showed. He was winding up to ask. She was sure of it. And she had a big fat yes ready to go at the tip of her tongue.

"What about college?"

"What about it?" She barely kept the exasperation out of her tone. Barely.

"Men there."

"You don't seem to mind asking personal questions."

"You don't seem to mind answering them."

"True."

"So?"

"One boyfriend."

"One." He didn't bother hiding his surprise. "Tell me about him."

"Why?"

"I want to know."

"Will this show up in one of your books?"

"Possibly."

She shot a look at the far wall of the restaurant, needing to escape the powerful eye contact with Beck, thinking about Dan and how to describe him, hoping her voice wouldn't thicken and betray tenderness. "He was full of energy and fun, always the center of a crowd, the life of the party. Everyone liked Dan."

He cocked his head quizzically. "Not everyone liked you?"

"I think people couldn't figure out what he was doing with me."

Oops. Should not have said that last part. But he was drawing her in with his sympathy and easy manner and she forgot to be a big fat liarpants. She couldn't even relax and coast on nodding and beaming because he wasn't talking about himself.

"What *was* he doing with you?"

Okay. She could fix this. She let her tongue creep out and take a leisurely exploratory voyage along her bottom lip. "Mmm…a lot of things."

The glass of champagne on the way to his lips froze before it reached its destination. May drained hers. Their food better come soon or she'd start bouncing up and down in her seat from excitement. Except for a few minor slipups, Veronica had taken over completely. May couldn't believe what she was saying, how she was acting. This was the most amazing thing she'd ever done, all the flirty silly stuff she'd watched other women doing, all the tricks Dan said a girl like her shouldn't bother trying to pull off—well, she was. Trying them. And pulling them off. And how.

George brought their first course, and after the first heavenly crunch, May set to in earnest, savoring the flavors mingling on her tongue before each next bite. Oh, the chef was a magician. And panko crumbs were her new passion. Light and crisp, they surrounded the juicy shrimp in an extraordinary non-greasy coating.

"Good?"

"Good." She smiled. Obviously the fact that she was inhaling crustaceans meant she thought it was good. "Now tell me about the women in your life."

He shrugged. "Seems I've always been with someone."

She stopped eating. He'd said that as if the concept utterly bored him. Was he with someone now? She'd never even thought to ask. *Yikes,* he could be married, too, though he didn't have a ring. "Always?"

"Well, not now."

She resumed breathing and went back to her meal.

"You talk about women as if they were interchangeable. Like Lego parts."

"No, nothing like that." He took a bite of purple lettuce and chewed thoughtfully. She waited, sensing the statement had a follow-up. "Actually…"

"They *are* Lego women?"

A frown creased his forehead. "Either love isn't all it's cracked up to be, or I'm not capable of it."

She rolled her eyes. "Don't tell me, let me guess. You think it should be a thrill a minute for the rest of your life."

His frown deepened, not as if her words upset him, but as if he was mulling them over. "No, I don't think it has to be. But something more than that feeling of déjà vu every time you get together."

She bit into her last shrimp and masticated it into panko-y pulp. Men. *Ptooey.* He sounded just like Dan. *Life isn't one big amusement park ride, boohoo.* "Maybe you haven't met the right woman."

"Maybe I haven't." He met her eyes deliberately across the table, and her panko pulp nearly went down the wrong pipe.

She put her fork down on her empty plate. "So you think there's a woman out there who can give you what you're looking for?"

"I'd like to believe there is."

May shook her head. "Maybe you need to be looking more at yourself."

"I don't understand."

"Are you as worried about making *her* life a thrill a minute?"

He didn't react, stared at her as if she'd suddenly materialized at his table for one.

Oops. May felt herself shrinking into familiar mortification. And he was doing exactly what Dan did when she screwed up. The old staring silent treatment. "I'm sor—"

"Maybe you're right."

She blinked. Maybe she was *what?* "I'm sorry?"

"I said maybe you're right."

May blinked again. She tried to think of one single time when Dan had admitted he was wrong. One. And was coming up empty all around. "Well I didn't mean to imply that—"

"Yes you did." He smiled, then his smile widened to a single-dimple chuckle. "Point well taken. I probably could have done more to keep the excitement going. I know I could have. Most of them had no problem telling me so."

George took their plates away, poured more champagne and left an awkward silence that May had to work not to squirm into.

So what now, Veronica? After that mess, a remark about the weather? A casual inquiry into the state of his book? A careless remark about the sex toys in your room, their use and function in times of—

"May."

"Yes?" She put an elbow on the table and rested her chin on the back of her hand, intending to look seductively all-ears, but instead feeling as if she was posing for one of those impossibly uncomfortable-looking professional head shots.

Damn. She'd been on such a roll, and then she got all earnest and analytical, more like her real self. For all his politeness, he was probably wondering how to cut the evening short. Get her statement on self-pleasuring for the Female Gender, then beat a hasty retreat to his room.

"Have you given any thought to helping me with my book?"

Bingo. Here it came. She'd have to pull a serious rabbit out of her hat to end the evening on the sensual note she'd been hoping for. "Of course."

"And?"

"I'm curious about one thing."

"What's that?"

"Why do you need me to tell you?"

He looked up from his champagne without lifting his head, so his eyes were half-lidded and sensual. "Let's just say the women I've known never seemed to feel the need to supplement."

"Ah." She tried to look as if she were absorbing the information calmly, all the while wanting to fan herself.

"So?"

"I'd love to help you." Her stomach clenched but she got the words out. Kept her face impassive. She reached for her bubbly and drained half of it, then caught his eye, which was looking rather speculative. *Uh-oh.*

"You're sure it doesn't bother you?"

"No, why?"

He frowned slightly. "I don't know, maybe the white knuckles holding your glass."

Damn. She put it down and gave him an *oh-pooh* wave. "Just making sure I don't drop it."

"Right. Okay."

He didn't believe her. Crap. She needed something to convince him. It was so important to her that she pull this off. After coming this far, she'd never forgive herself if she backed out of the chance to get so intimate and sexual with this gorgeous man.

"So how did you want to proceed?" She stifled a

groan. Maybe she could sound a little more like a textbook.

"You can write down your thoughts, or…"

"Mmm?"

"You can tell me here, or…" He looked around. "Somewhere more private."

That sounded more interesting. Except she could feel a blush zooming up her cheeks, and he was giving her that skeptical look of concern again, as if he was pushing the dainty flower beyond her abilities. Damn damn *damn*.

She had to show him this dainty flower could kick serious butt.

"Those would be fine…" May trailed off, then hesitated deliberately.

"But?"

"But I was wondering…" She leaned forward as if she was afraid of being overheard, when actually, she wanted to give him a lovely long look down her dress.

"Wondering?" Instead of down her dress, he was looking concerned again, and her heart gave a thump.

"If instead of me writing down my views on the subject…" She leaned farther.

"Yes?" This time his eyes did make the journey. And stayed for a nice long visit.

"Or telling you what they are…"

"Ye-e-es?"

She raised her eyebrows, all innocence.

"I wondered if you'd rather just watch me."

6

Note on Exhibit A waitstaff board:

One of our performers, Sasha, lost an earring. Silver stud with dangling pearl drop. Please keep an eye out.
Frank

MAY CLOSED the room door behind her and slumped against it as if bad guys were chasing her and she'd barely managed to give them the slip. Oh, my God, what had she *done?* Told Beck she'd pleasure herself in front of him? While he watched? And what, took *notes?*

Oh, my God.

The second the offer had left her lips, even Veronica had freaked out. It was all she could do to keep the sensual expression on her face while her nerve endings were crackling and zinging in terror. One thing to flirt and smolder appropriately. But she was hardly a sexual dominatrix. Dan had always taken the lead in the bedroom. She'd never had to perform for anyone like this.

Somehow she'd made it through the rest of the delicious meal. Somehow, she'd managed to chat normally—granted he was interesting and seemed interested in what she thought and felt, which she wasn't used to since Dan knew her so well he didn't need to ask anymore. Somehow, she managed a smile when the elevator reached his floor and he got off alone. She needed to freshen up, she'd said. She'd be by his room in a bit.

A bit? Could she psych herself up for something like this in a *bit?* She didn't even think she could do it in a huge honking chunk.

As far as she could tell, none of her dinner had digested yet; it was all sitting right there in her stomach, exactly as swallowed.

May sank down on the bed, hugging her arms around her. Oh, what she wouldn't give right now to be back in Oshkosh in her cozy, safe apartment, with Dan stretched out beside her, watching TV or begging for a backrub, *Pleeeeeeez, May? I'll give you one later....* Only somehow he never got around to it more than a couple of times a year.

She pictured his tanned skin, his stocky body, the curves of his strong muscles softened by the few pounds he'd put on in the last few years. She knew every inch of that body.

The longing increased and she lunged for the phone, dialed the number she knew so well and waited, breathless. This would be a sign. If he was home, if he sounded at all like he missed her, she'd cancel Masturbation 101 and go back to Oshkosh tomorrow. But if he—

"Hello?"

A woman's voice. May sat up ramrod straight. "Is this 555-5237?"

"Yes. Who's this?"

In the background she could hear Dan's voice asking the same question.

"This is May. I'm calling from New York. Can I speak to Dan?"

The line made a fumbling muted sound, as if the woman had put her hand over the mouthpiece, though only partially because May could still hear. "It's May. She's in New York. Why is she calling you?"

"What's she doing in New York?" Dan's voice sounded louder, incredulous. "Give me the phone."

"Dan's not available right now." The woman's tone turned sickly sweet.

"I can hear him." May squeezed a handful of the turned-down bedspread without mercy. "Who is this?"

"This is his *girlfriend*, Charlene."

Shouting from Dan, answering screeches from Charlene.

May's breath rushed into her lungs and refused to come back out. Girlfriend? Already? It took Dan six months of dating May before he'd allow the word.

More fumbling on the line—a tussle for the phone? Then a squeal of outrage from Charlene, whoever the hell she was, which meant Dan must have gained possession. Thank goodness.

"May, where are you?"

His familiar voice brought tears to—

Wait a second. Tears? What the hell for? She blinked ferociously. "I'm in New York."

"Where in New York? What are you doing there?" He sounded agitated and off balance, which suited her just fine.

"At Hush Hotel. Look it up. It's not the kind of place you stay alone." May slammed down the receiver and jumped to her feet. Strode to the desk, whirled around and strode back to the bed.

Dan had a girlfriend. They didn't even know anyone named…

Wait a second. Charlene...

May fisted her hands. The woman with dark hair and megahooters crammed into a tight T-shirt who'd been all over him when they went to the Dobsons' for dinner in February. Soon after, the broken dates, days in a row without seeing him, promised phone calls that never materialized, the sullen behavior and dissatisfaction. May thought he was just having a midtwenties crisis.

More like a perky D-cup crisis.

The creep. The double, triple, quadruple, stinking, economy-size creep.

She wanted a sign? She just got one whole hell of one.

No more looking back. She'd freshen up, change, check out the marital aids in the drawer next to the bed and see which ones would do for the sex show of a lifetime.

Then she'd go to Beck's room, rip off her clothes and pleasure the freaking hell out of herself.

BECK CLOSED the door of his room and leaned back against it. How was he going to handle this? For all her willingness to help him, May was clearly panicked even by the thought of what she insisted she wanted to do.

He pushed himself away from the door and took a few steps forward, put his hands on his hips and frowned at the extra long queen-size bed. Why put herself through this if it wasn't something she was comfortable with? She didn't strike him as the type who'd frolic through hell to please a man. She seemed much stronger than that. But why would a woman willing to shack up for a week in an erotic boutique hotel with a married man she'd just met balk at putting it out there for a different stranger, one she was clearly attracted to?

Faced with her crisis of confidence, or whatever it

was, he probably should have withdrawn the offer. But, perversely, her insistence in the face of obvious discomfort fascinated him. He wanted to see how she conducted herself, see what other peeks into May Ellison's psyche he might be allowed.

And yes, he also wanted to see if Alex was right about what would improve the scene, or whether Beck knew his characters and books and readers better than she did. Which he'd bet turned out to be the case. He strode to the room phone and dialed the concierge.

"Good evening, Mr. Desmond, how can I help you?"

"I'd like a dozen candles and a basket of rose petals sent up as soon as possible."

"Yes, sir, right away."

He hung up the phone, smiling. Only at HUSH. There was probably nothing they hadn't been asked to produce at a moment's notice.

Now, to set the stage. Adrenaline pumping, he moved the exquisite chocolate mint from his pillow to his nightstand and pulled up the neatly turned-down gold patterned bedspread. Changed the classical station the evening maid left his radio tuned to, so soft jazz filled the room. He hoped May liked jazz; he hadn't asked her.

Add it to the growing list of things he wondered about her. It was hard to get her talking about herself. She tended to answer questions with bare facts or evasions or turned the conversation back at him.

Obviously she wanted to stay as anonymous and private as possible, which was her right. But he wanted to know more. Get to understand her contrasts, figure out her moods.

He rolled his eyes. He should be obsessing more about

the book and less about May. Not like him to let anything come between his concentration and a writing issue.

A gentle knock on the room door shot nerves through him, and he chuckled incredulously. When was the last time he'd been nervous about meeting a woman? And this wasn't even a date, it was…research.

He threw himself a look of disgust in the bathroom mirror. Right. And seeing her naked touching herself was going to be a completely clinical experience.

Changing the look of disgust into a warm smile to welcome her, he opened the door…to a member of the concierge staff bearing candles, a box of HUSH matches and a small basket of pink rose petals. In his book they were red, but pink would do. In fact, it would complement May's skin tone even better.

The attractive young woman smiled, accepted his tip and his thanks, and closed the door behind her. Beck rushed to distribute the candles around the room, lit them and turned off the electric lights, glad the props had arrived so he could set the scene before May got here, to decrease any anxiety she might still be feeling. The petals he'd save to scatter over her no-doubt fabulous body during the main event.

Perfect. He smiled in satisfaction. The candles glowed and made the rich wood of the bed gleam, threw mysterious flickering shadows on the walls. Alex thought the masturbation scene in his book was straight out of a porn movie? He was about to prove how wrong she was. Some people were uptight, sexually repressed; for all Alex's brassiness, maybe she was conservative in the bedroom.

Another knock on the door, this one not so gentle. He fought down the rush of excitement and opened the door calmly, determined to make sure May didn't regret her offer to help.

"Hello, May."

She looked beautiful—when did she not?—and walked past him into the room, carrying a small bag. She'd changed from the sexy black dress to an equally sexy tight black off-shoulder top that left her firm mid-riff bare, and a fire-engine red clingy short skirt that hugged her round hips adoringly.

Research. Right.

"Thanks for coming."

"I haven't yet, but you're welcome. The candles are beautiful." She turned to him, and whatever uncertainty had been plaguing her before was history now. She was on fire, cheeks flushed, eyes bright and sure. A female work of art. He was suddenly unsure which of them would need putting at ease.

"Would you like a drink?"

"No, thanks."

"Would you feel more comfortable if we chatted first, or—"

She held up a hand to stop him. Tipped her chin and gave him one of those killer sultry stares. "Let's just do it, Beck."

Her soft words had the opposite effect on his penis. He needed to focus on the scene, focus on his book. If he nearly lost it when she spoke to him, he was lunch meat when she took off her clothes. Hard salami to be precise.

"Good." He gestured to a chair a few feet from the bed. "Okay if I sit here?"

"No problem."

He sat and took out his laptop. "Do you mind if I take notes?"

"Knock yourself out."

She stood still for a moment, facing him, staring at the floor. Then put her hands to the hem of her shirt, and lifted it slowly, steadily, exposing her full round breasts, captured—barely it seemed—in a few inches of black lace, nipples clearly visible under the sheer fabric.

Oh my—

Beck's hands froze on the keyboard, along with his thoughts. The music shifted to a more upbeat tune and May swayed her hips dreamily along with the beat, ran her hands up the sides of her body, cupped her breasts and lifted them, a swelling, generous offering.

He managed to type a few phrases, fingers stumbling over the keys. This was perfect. This was exactly the kind of action he had in his scene already. Oh, he of little faith. Take that, all ye who doubted him.

May put her hands on the waistband of her skirt and lowered it, inch by tantalizing inch off her beautiful hips, exposing tiny black lace bikini underwear. She threw the skirt dramatically to one side, where it landed in a scarlet heap on the edge of the black desk.

Perfect, perfect, perfect. He couldn't wait to tell Alex. He wouldn't have to change a single word.

She fell back on the bed, undulating her body in an imitation of the sex act.

"Wait." He lunged out of his seat, grabbed the basket of petals and sprinkled them on her already rosy body, head to toe. Yes. *Yes*. They decorated and framed her just as he'd imagined the red ones decorating and framing Tamara's slightly darker skin. He took his seat again, practically rubbing his hands in delight.

May picked up a petal, dragged it across her lip, across her breasts, grabbed a handful and sprinkled them deliberately over her sex, so they lay like a pink flower bed between her legs.

Wow. He wanted to call Alex right now and told-you-so her into submission. Moreover, he was completely in control of himself now, aroused, sure, but nothing he couldn't handle. This was such a damn good idea.

With sensual, tantalizing slowness, May reached into the bag she'd brought with her and pulled out a large pink dildo.

He could only stare. Had she read the scene?

She drew the phallus across her face, mouth open as if she was longing for a suck. Her right hand made its way into her bra, she pulled out one breast, then the other, pinched the nipples roughly to stand upright, her eyes wide-open and staring.

Yes. Yes. Yes.

Her hand slipped down over her panties, drew them aside so he could see the lips and crevices of her sex, soft and sweetly clean of hair. Oh, yes.

She pushed the dildo down, the unlubricated silicone catching and stuttering across her stomach. The tip teased her opening; she arched her back, moaned loudly, pushed again, harder, forcing the huge molded penis inside her.

Her moans didn't sound quite right. Not quite sincere. Her brow furrowed at the same time his did. She pulled the inch of rubber out and tried again. This time she grimaced openly.

Beck stopped typing.

She tried again, eyes screwed shut. Air rushed in through her clenched teeth. Pain.

God he was a fool.

He placed his laptop on the table, shot up out of the

chair and took the toy from her clenched fingers. "Stop."

May opened startled eyes, then yanked her underpants back into place and sat up abruptly, shoving her breasts back into her bra. "That's all you needed?"

He sat on the bed. What an ass, what a total idiot he'd been. She wasn't masturbating. She was putting on a show, what she thought he wanted to see. She didn't even know to lubricate the dildo.

"Is that how you do it when you're alone?" He asked as gently as he knew how, not wanting to humiliate her.

She bit her lip, worldly sophisticate aura gone as if it was paint washed away in a turpentine storm. "No."

Tears glinted in the eyes she lowered to the bed. Whatever kind of ass he felt like before, he felt like even more of one now, and whatever tenderness he'd experienced tripled.

He pushed a lock of hair off her forehead, watched it fall back down. May flinched away. No sympathy wanted; he could understand her pride. "That was very sexy."

She managed a brief smile.

"You'd drive any guy out of his mind. I'm serious."

A brief nod; she was clearly not buying it.

"It was a lot like the scene I have already in my book. The striptease, the candles, rose petals and toys. I want to see it real, May."

"Real?"

His turn to nod. "I want to see the real you."

The words left his mouth and he realized with a small shock they were true of more than her masturbation technique. She lifted her head, gaze hopeful, as if he'd said something profound and freeing.

He touched her cheek, letting his hand linger as long as he dared. "Think about it."

May sucked in a breath, stared down at her meshed fingers. "I'll do it."

"Only if you want to."

"I do."

He wasn't convinced. "Maybe another night would be—"

"Please." She spoke quietly, lifting those gorgeous blue eyes to his. "I want to do this."

He gazed at her, at the combination of courage and vulnerability, and an ache started in the center of his chest. He had a crazy impulse to lean down and kiss her until she smiled in genuine happiness, to curl her up in his arms and sleep with her until morning.

What the hell was that?

"You're sure you want to?"

"I'm sure." She pursed her lips and sent him an apologetic glance. "It's not very exciting."

He grinned. "I'll be the judge of that."

"Okay." She grinned back, then laughed nervously. "It's a deal."

He took her hand, played lightly with her fingers. "One thing I want to ask first. Why did you do it for me the other way?"

"I...thought it's what you expected."

"It was what I expected." He squeezed her fingers and let go. "But apparently it wasn't what I wanted."

She shrugged, and for a second he saw again the battle in her eyes and wanted to step in and save her from it. But before he'd opened his mouth to give her another out, she blinked and straightened her shoulders. "Okay. I'm ready."

He gave in, went back to his chair, lifted his computer back onto his lap and waited, not at all sure what to expect, caught between diminishing concern for his book and increasing concern for May.

She lay back, stared at the ceiling, a long breath in, a long breath out. He could see her body relaxing, starting with her feet, which flopped to the side, then the muscles in her legs, releasing tension, thighs, abdomen, shoulders, chin, until her forehead smoothed and her eyes lazily closed.

He hardly dared breathe, not even sure why his anticipation was so much stronger this time, why his instinct was on high-alert for something unexpected.

Slowly, she arched her back and moved her hands under, unhooked her bra and slid the straps off each shoulder, and tossed it to the foot of the bed. Then lay for another few seconds, not moving at all. Her breasts were beautiful, small nipples standing proudly, her skin inviting shades of cream and gold and rose.

He swallowed, his throat convulsing.

The music changed to a slow, dreamy number, "I've Got You Under My Skin," alto sax evoking a tobacco-throated blues singer.

May lifted her hips, slid her lace panties down the gorgeous smooth length of her legs and tossed them aside. Lay back again, motionless, her legs casually apart, a tiny strip of curling hair at the juncture, everything else smooth and pink.

His cock started getting hard. She was beyond beautiful—ethereal—breathing peacefully, naked on his bed about to bring herself to orgasm…he'd never live through it.

She lifted one hand, drew it languidly up her stomach, trailing fingers passing lightly over each breast, then continuing the circle back. Up and down. Up and down, closer to her sex with each pass. Her toes pointed, then relaxed, pointed and held.

Again her hand slid down, this time stopped just short of the soft-looking neatly shaped tangle of hair. He mentally urged her on, exhaling sharply in frustration when her hand caressed its way back up to her breasts and fondled them gently. A tiny smile touched her mouth; her palm glided back down, hesitated under her navel, then finally—oh, yes—she slipped her fingers between her legs.

He shifted back in the plush black chair, fully erect. May spread her legs wide, bent at the knees. Beck put his laptop aside. Screw note-taking. There wasn't a chance in hell he'd forget one second of this.

She stroked a long, slender finger down the center of her sex, then up again, taking her time, teasing herself, making him crazy until he could barely sit still. And could barely suppress a moan when the length of that finger disappeared inside her, in, out, in, out, then reappeared fully to spread glistening wetness around the surrounding deep pink lips, and up onto her clitoris.

Torture.

He attempted to shift his erection to a more comfortable position from where it strained painfully against the seam of his pants. No luck. It wanted a hell of a lot more than comfort.

The finger on her clit started a light, steady circle; her nostrils flared, her lips parted, her breath came higher and faster.

Beck moved again on the seat, bracing himself for what he was about to see, barely under control. This was it.

The circles stopped; he swallowed a groan. Her hand moved back up to caress her breasts, dipped back down to stroke her sex briefly, then away again.

He'd been so desperately wrong. She was making love to herself the way a woman wanted to be made love to. Building slowly, teasing, tantalizing, to the peak of arousal. What he'd written was a fantasy of male screwing, a huge phallus pounded in hard. Alex had been right.

May found her clit again, rubbed in more earnest circles; her head rose off the pillow then hit back down. A flush broke over her face and her chest; she let out a soft moan. Getting close.

Her orgasm was going to kill him.

He held himself in his seat, every instinct yelling at him to lunge onto the bed, bury his face between her legs to taste her ravenously, make her come, then while she was still climaxing, plunge furiously inside her and take his own pleasure.

He couldn't. Wouldn't. But it took all his strength to resist.

She moaned again, her pelvis tilted upward, the circles she drew with her clit grew larger, harder, faster, frantic.

He gave in—at least partway. Unzipped his pants and, half-ashamed, grabbed his cock to match her rhythm, straining for his own climax as she strained for hers.

She relaxed suddenly; her mouth opened in a silent "oh." Her breath went in and in and in, then her hips rose off the bed, scattering pink petals; she cried out and thrashed, cried out again, tense, breathless, panting.

He grabbed a tissue from the lacquer box on the table next to him and his own orgasm hit hard; he caught the semen, wave after wave, then shuddered out the last drops and slumped back in his chair.

May lay still, eyes closed, limp, sated, breathing fast and deep; he wasn't sure she realized what she'd driven him to, or that he was even in the room for that matter.

Another tissue, and a third, he cleaned himself up, zipped his pants, hands unsteady, brain reeling.

Holy shit.

Her eyes opened at the zipper sound; she smiled at him, flushed, gorgeous, languid. "How was that?"

He meant to laugh, but couldn't, shook his head instead. "I don't think I've ever seen anything sexier in my life."

"No?" She got up on one elbow, watching him curiously; he probably looked as stunned and spent as he felt.

"No." He held her darkened blue gaze, and something sprang to life between them that deepened the intimacy to an almost unbearable degree.

May blinked and looked away, retrieved her underwear calmly and put it on with steady hands—hadn't she felt it?—panties first, bra next, then her clothes, as relaxed and natural in his room as she'd been tense and out of her element before.

Would he ever figure her out?

"Thank you for doing this." He wanted to laugh at himself, at the earnest Boy Scout way the words came out.

But he was beyond grateful. The scene for his book would come alive in a way he'd never have anticipated and he knew he'd be up most of the night trying to capture what she'd shown him on paper, sure without doubt this was what Alex had meant, what she'd known was missing and he was too duh-male to get. He'd happily eat crow if he could manage to portray even some of what May had shared with him.

"You're welcome." She put on the rest of her clothes and dropped the pink sex toy back into her bag. He wondered if he should ask her to stay, but she was already moving toward the door.

Then she stopped and turned back. "Can I ask you…"

"Sure." He took three steps toward her, until he was a foot away, close enough to touch her, or kiss her. "Ask away. Whatever you want."

"Did you come just now?"

He grinned. "As if I hadn't in weeks."

She laughed, pressed her lips together as if she shouldn't have, then laughed again. "I'm glad."

"Why?"

"Because it's more fun with two."

"Very true." That was his cue. *Let's make it both of us together next time.* But for some reason, the words wouldn't come.

Instead, he gestured to his laptop, on the black desk where her scarlet skirt had lain a minute before. "I'd ask you to stay for a drink, but I have plenty to keep me busy tonight, thanks to you."

"That's okay." If she was disappointed by the lack of invitation, she didn't show it. "It's been a long day, I should get to bed."

He followed her to the door, reached over her head to hold it open, feeling like something still needed to be done or said to make the night complete, but unsure what it was.

"Well…" She turned under his arm and smiled again, peaceful and triumphant. "Good night."

"Good night."

She started to move out of his room, and he took hold of her arm, not ready to let her go, and not even sure why.

May turned back questioningly.

Without a clue he was going to, he leaned down and kissed her.

Her lips were soft and warm; she inhaled sharply and stilled in his doorway. Unable to keep himself from her once he'd started, he kissed her again, and again. This time she responded and he let the door close behind her, gathered her in his arms and let the taste of her mouth fill him, her scent fill him, the feel of her body fill him up. She tasted sweet, smelled like sex and roses, and felt like his fantasy woman come true.

Then he let her go, because what the hell was he doing kissing her like a crazy-in-love fool?

She took a step back, wearing a soft, vulnerable, happy look that undid him, though he was pretty undone to begin with.

He opened the door, leaned in and kissed her again. "Good night, May. I'll see you tomorrow."

She whispered good-night and walked out of the room. He let the door close behind her and stared at it, reliving the kiss over and over like a schoolboy who'd just had his first one, unable to understand how the touch of a virtual stranger's mouth could have filled him so completely, and how he could have gone this long without realizing or understanding how empty he was before.

7

Note on Concierge board:

*Are we giving the jewelry to Trevor's babe today?
Though I must say, this one looks a lot nicer than
the others. Usually bimbo central in that room.*
Linda

Reply on Concierge board:

*We haven't heard not to. And you're right, this
woman actually looks like the type who deserves
Tiffany. She smiles, says thank-you and tips!
Though after the lucky stiff got to have dinner
with Beck Desmond last night, I'm not sure she de-
serves anything.*
Moira
(Grinning evilly)

MAY FINISHED the last crisp crumbs of her *pain au chocolat,* found an overlooked plump raspberry at the bottom
of her fresh fruit bowl, wiped her mouth with the linen napkin and drained the last drop of an excellent pot of coffee.

Breakfast served in bed should be a daily occurrence.
An elegant breakfast, like this one, eaten at nearly ten

after a long, sound sleep and a long dishy chat with Ginny, recapping only the details from her date May felt comfortable sharing. None of this 7:00 a.m. cornflakes and wheat germ dutifully shoveled in at the kitchen table, one eye on the clock so as not to be late for work.

She pushed the tray out of the way and swung her legs off the bed, stood and stretched contentedly, arms way up, muscles lengthening. *Ahhhh.* What indulgence to dally in now? How to make herself feel even more luxurious and pampered?

A knock on the door and the muffled announcement of a concierge staff member seemed perfectly timed. What magnificence was about to arrive?

A smiling young woman proffered a small distinctive blue box with a blue bow May recognized as being from Tiffany & Co., her father's store of choice—or was it Mom's?—for special occasion jewelry. May thanked her and the woman left, still smiling, as if working at HUSH was equivalent to an all-day orgasm. Or did they just give the staff uppers?

She turned, holding the box, eyeing it curiously. From Trevor. It had to be from Trevor. But even telling herself that twice didn't stop the disappointment when she saw the card. "For a very lovely and talented lady, Trevor."

Ew. She rolled her eyes and held the box at arm's length. Should she even bother opening it, or just have them put it back in the "Trevor closet" with the other thousand or so boxes waiting their turn to be presented to other lovely and *talented—blech—*ladies?

On the other hand, Tiffany was Tiffany, and this was May's adventure, and Trevor deserved having the price of whatever was inside deducted from his sleazy bulging wallet.

She pulled off the ribbon and opened the box, which contained a silver serpentine bangle. May slid the cool smooth metal over her wrist and laughed. Very fitting that the bracelet should evoke a snake. It was lovely, but…well, who cared?

She put the bracelet back in the box and closed the lid, doubting she'd even be able to take it home with her. That kind of souvenir she didn't want.

Last night when she'd come back from Beck's room—okay, floated back—and undressed, a rose petal had fallen out of her bra and drifted to the ground. She'd gathered it up and, fully recognizing that she was being a sentimental fool, pressed it between two tissues in the pages of the volume of erotica she found in a drawer. As far as she was concerned, that little petal was worth ten times whatever this bracelet cost, even though Beck had only been setting the scene for his novel, and the petal meant as much to him as the bracelet meant to Trevor.

Except…Beck had come to her rescue in such a sweet way after that dismal start last night—how people ever got those giant rubber dicks inside them, she hadn't a clue. And that sweet rescue had started May on a slippery slope to some gooey thinking that was way dangerous in this situation. In one corner, Big Famous Devastatingly Handsome Author researching a scene. And in the other? Rebounding Rita, ripe for falling for the first man who smiled at her.

More than smiled. Said in that gentle deep voice that he wanted to see the real her. He could not have picked a more perfect thing to say to Ms. May Ellison. Even though she knew he was talking about sex, her traitorous Wisconsin May-bes had wasted no time jumping in for some fun. Maybe he really cared about her. Maybe he'd glimpsed her true self and wanted at it. Maybe he wouldn't be bored or turned off by her as she really was. Maybe he had romance in the back of his mind, and not just commercial fiction.

Sometimes she exasperated the hell out of herself.

But his words had relaxed and emboldened her enough to do what three days ago she never would have imagined she'd be able to. Lose herself enough in front of a near-stranger to be able to bring herself off.

She frowned and headed to the bathroom to brush her teeth. "Lose herself" wasn't the right phrase. The entire time she'd been so aware of him, straining to hear sounds from his chair, wanting so much to sneak a peek. Was he watching? Turned-on? Or, God forbid, typing away, bored and yawning?

In her closed-eyes fantasy, he was going wild for her. By the time she was close to coming, she'd been frantic for him to get up off the damn chair and make love to her—or hell, even screw her—until they went over the edge together.

But of course, that was fantasy, and fantasies didn't come true often. She *had* excited him enough to take care of himself, thank goodness. But he wasn't after sex, let alone her hyperromantic vision of attraction leading to love, marriage, babies and fiftieth anniversary parties.

So…how to explain that kiss?

May raised her head and stared at her dreamy-eyed expression in the bathroom mirror, toothpaste foam ringing her lips, while thrills played tag all over her body.

If men kissed women like that simply because they were grateful for help on their books, then she was able to turn dildos into *pain au chocolat* by winking at them.

She spit out a mouthful of toothpaste. *Whoa Nelly, them's some dangerous thoughts there.* Ginny, of course, had May and Beck halfway to being engaged already, and May hadn't told her about the scene in the bedroom, and had played way down her reaction to the kiss. But even without Ginny's help, she was poised, very un-Veronica-like, on the brink of serious infatuation. Even if there was the smallest germ of truth to her wishful thoughts, with only three full days of her stay left, including today, nothing could come of the attraction. There simply wasn't time. Forget that the more she saw of him the more she wanted to have another week, or two, or three, to see what happened.

What should she do? Pursue him? Back off? Wait until he made the next move? Ginny thought she should go all out, but Ginny was in it for the vicarious celebrity romance thrill and didn't understand the danger May's heart might be in.

May sighed, wiped her mouth with a thick HUSH towel and tossed her toothbrush to rattle back into the glass. Who was she kidding? She was acting as if this could be a normal romance. Was she forgetting that he thought she was Veronica? That their little dalliance, however it turned out, belonged firmly in the fantasy thrill column?

How about she stopped analyzing and worrying over every tiny little nuance of everything that happened to her and just *live?*

Ya think, May?

She showered, dressed in a blue-and-white short clingy sundress, put on light makeup and considered her options for the day's activities.

The city beckoned, wasn't that what cities were supposed to do? As much as going out on her own made her nervous, she couldn't stay inside the hotel the entire week. Even an amazing hotel like this one. She'd come all the way to New York, the city her mother had told her so much about; now that she wasn't spending all day in bed with Trevor—and thank God for that— she should at least see some of it.

At the room's window, she pulled back the curtain. Gray clouds glided by overhead; down below wind swirled trash on the sidewalks and threatened pedestrian hairstyles. Not ideal weather to venture out in.

But really, she couldn't sit in the room all day. Especially because if she knew herself, she'd be brooding way worse than she had been already, secretly or not-so-secretly waiting and hoping for the phone to ring. At someone's *beck* and call as it were. She'd done too many years of that with Dan. It was time to be her *own* woman, whoever that turned out to be today. May, Veronica, or some combination thereof. Dan was doing Charlene back home in Oshkosh, and May was here without him, ready to go.

She added a light blue cotton sweater to the sundress and marched to the elevators, through the lobby—no signs of Eartha Kitty today—and out the door, held open for her by today's supermodel-slash-doorman.

The temperature was much hotter than seemed possible for a cloudy day, air heavy with coming rain; the wind blew unpleasantly warm and smelly, like a giant's bad breath. Not a day for endless aimless wandering with no umbrella. But a brief stroll down Madison Avenue would be possible. Just to say she'd done it. She could explore farther this afternoon, or tomorrow. If she felt up to it.

Half a block later, the oppressive air made the

sweater unbearable and she took it off, nearly punching an old man in the process. How did anyone tolerate all these bodies wherever he or she went? Pushing past, hurrying, dodging; the crush made her even more breathless than the ninety-nine percent humidity.

She waited at the corner of Madison and East 41st until the light changed, the giant's bad breath threatening to blow her skirt up. One step into the street she had to jump back to avoid being run over by a taxi swinging around the corner, horn blaring, driver shouting something she doubted was a compliment.

Lovely. Would she ever get the hang of this city? How had her mother tolerated it? What had appealed?

A shop window caught her eye and drew her over as if the contents were magnetized. An art supply store. She hesitated only a second and went inside. A few minutes later, she emerged, unscathed, clutching a beautiful set of colored pencils and a lightweight collapsible easel, much nicer than the one she had at home.

Well, that was cool. Maybe she just needed a positive experience like that to kick her in the right direction.

Vastly cheered and encouraged, she managed three steps north on Madison when the rain chose that precise moment to begin falling—no, pelting—in heavy drops that splattered the sidewalk with circles the size of quarters until no dry surface remained.

May turned and ran for the safety of the HUSH lobby. She waited there a few minutes, air cold on her damp skin, watching the streaking rain, a lucky few pedestrians producing umbrellas or newspapers to hold over their heads.

So much for her first wild woman exploration of the city. Eartha Kitty regarded her from a chair in the lobby

with her usual contempt, and May had a fairly uncharacteristic desire to give sweet little pussums the finger.

Back in the elevator, she contemplated the buttons,
scowling. Back to her room? To do what, pace? Watch
TV? After her brave decision to venture out, that seemed
a horrible surrender.

The elevator doors slid shut at the same time she saw
the button for the roof garden and pressed it reflexively.
There were bowers up there where she could sit protected from the rain and draw. And maybe Clarissa
would be there; it would be nice to see a friendly face
and have someone to chat with.

On the roof level, she got off and pushed through the
doors to find the freak shower had stopped. The sky was
still gray, but the breeze was much cooler, and the fresh,
earthy smells of a wet garden beckoned her out into it.
Incredibly, a red-tailed hawk that had been sitting on the
edge of the roof took off at her approach and flapped
leisurely across the street to perch on the roof opposite.

That was probably one of the last things she'd expect
to see in the middle of any city, let alone one this size.
She set up her easel and did several sketches from different angles. The first, of an espaliered apple tree,
framed by the similar artifice of the buildings behind it.
Second, of a fancy topiary contrasted with the natural
fall of an overflowing box of nasturtiums.

Finally, a sketch of the part of the garden the hawk
had been in, a tub of blue spruce, a cedar, black-eyed
Susans and daylilies, a tiny still-wet stone cherub with
a tear-shaped mossy stain on his face, which reminded
her of Leonardo, the whimsical stone turtle in her mom's
backyard. As a final touch, she drew in the hawk, still

visible across the street, sketching him perched on the wrist of the stone child, as if they were lifelong friends.

There.

She flipped the sketch pad closed and folded up the easel, satisfied and feeling more grounded. A new path toward part of the garden she hadn't seen on her previous visit enticed her in that direction.

She stepped around a pair of arbor vitae sandwiching a streaming statue of David, and found Clarissa, apparently untouched by the violent shower, pruning shears in hand, dealing with a dripping tangle of morning glory vines that had extended beyond their allotted place on an iron fence and were encroaching on an extensive vegetable garden.

"Hi." May smiled at the older woman, feeling like she had a friend, even after only one encounter.

"Oh, have you been painting?"

"Just sketching."

"I'd love to see what you've done."

"Oh." May glanced doubtfully down at her sketch pad; she was generally pretty private about her work. "None of them are finished…"

"Perhaps later, then. You're just in time, I'm about done with these morning glories, then I'll need help planting lettuce. You game?"

"Sure." May beamed. Another thing she felt at home doing. A red-letter day. "How do you get your morning glories blooming so early? Are you that much ahead here? In Wisconsin it's late July or August before they flower."

"I start them inside. They grow so quickly." She snipped off the tip of a vine reaching for a nearby basket of impatiens. "Did you know that sweet potatoes are the root of a certain type of morning glory?"

"No, I didn't." May stooped to pick up the cuttings, shook off the drips, and put them into the basket already containing an assortment of other prunings.

"Amazing little things." Clarissa looked at a blossom admiringly. "So pretty. And only out for one day. One morning, really. They have to make the most of it."

May caught her sidelong glance. Was that today's lesson? "Very wise."

"Indeed. I'm finished here. Come along, I've already prepared the soil."

She swept over to a long narrow bed of freshly raked soil, glistening brown from the brief storm, and handed May a pair of rubber-dipped cotton gloves and a packet of assorted lettuce seeds, which she'd pulled from the pocket of her strawberry print apron. "I sow lettuce every two weeks so the restaurant always has a fresh supply."

"You do this all yourself?"

"Oh, no. Usually I have Rosa to help, but she's gone off to get married." Clarissa gestured with her gloved hand toward half of the bed. "Here, this is your spot, I'll do over there."

May nodded obediently, and knelt on the dry cushion Clarissa handed her. She carefully poured the tiny seeds into her hand and began sowing them in rows eight inches apart.

"Now, May, tell me how your week is going without Mr. Little."

May grinned at the command, issued with all the aplomb of a queen. Yet, somehow May didn't mind opening up to this woman she'd just met. "Probably better than it would have with him."

"I dare say." Clarissa paused for a wink and a smile. "And dinner last night with the handsome and talented Beck Desmond."

"Yes." May didn't even bother questioning how Clarissa knew. "He seems very nice."

"He is." Clarissa continued serenely putting out lettuce seeds. "And a hot hunk of beefcake to boot."

May burst out laughing. "You might say that."

And a damn good kisser. She pulled on the gloves, crumbled a layer of wet soil over the seeds and moved on to the next row, hoping her blush wasn't too obvious.

"Are there other adventurers in your family? Or are you the first?"

"Oh, I'm not the first." May smiled, a little relieved at the change of subject. Next she would have found herself telling Clarissa about the scene in Beck's bedroom. "My mother left Wisconsin and came to New York in her twenties. She'd always dreamed of being a Rockette."

"And?"

"And she became one. For a while."

"Until…"

May smiled and patted the soil firm. "Until my father, then her ex-boyfriend, came after her. He got tickets to her show and sat in the front row. Went backstage afterwards and told her to pack her bags, that now she'd gotten adventure out of her system, they were going back to Wisconsin to get married."

Clarissa held her seeds suspended over their intended target. "And did she?"

May nodded dreamily. She loved imagining the scene, had done so over and over from the first time she heard the story. Her father, grim, handsome, determined and uncomfortable in the theater surroundings. Her mother, young, leggy and vivacious, realizing her mistake and deciding to come home to the reality of love. "They've been happily married for fifty-two years."

"That's a lovely story." Clarissa's seeds sprinkled down onto the soil; she watched them fall but made no move to cover them over. "I was married for forty-one years, also very happily."

May sat back on her heels, not sure how much she could ask, but wanting the story. "How did you meet your husband?"

"I was engaged to someone else at the time, rather late in life for back then, I was twenty-seven. But to my parents' despair, I was in no hurry to settle down or settle at all, as I saw it then."

"What do you mean?"

"Love seemed such an imperfect concept. All the thrills at the beginning, all the surprises, then inevitably the slow decline into predictability and disenchantment."

Something cold and heavy landed in the pit of May's stomach and she fought it with the heat of denial. "Does it have to be that way?"

"Of course not." Clarissa dismissed the concept with a wave. "It's just what I thought. So while I was engaged to this terribly respectable young attorney my parents adored, I did the unexpected, which, given who I was at the time, was actually fairly typical. I fell madly in love with their new young gardener. We eloped, everyone was scandalized, it was delightful. He went on to law school and became a fine lawyer. I adored him as much at the end as I did at the beginning. Probably more."

"Even without the thrills and surprises?"

"Oh, there were always thrills and surprises." The sad, faraway look in her eyes made May's heart ache. "Just not quite as many quite so close together as there were in the beginning. But you don't have to give those up. You shouldn't in fact. That would be settling of the worst kind."

May thought of Dan, of the comforting peace of their routine and how she'd cherished it. Yet…there had been moments of feeling disconnected, nagging doubts that had crept in once in a while. Was this really all there was and would be? She'd never been with anyone else, how would she know? And yet she'd loved him…so she stayed, even when it felt like a habit.

"That's a wonderful story."

"Yes." Clarissa briskly got back to planting. "Jim died three years ago. I gave up the house in Connecticut and moved into our apartment in the city. You must come to tea while you're here. Tomorrow afternoon, I'll send you the address."

"Thank you." May smiled warmly, telling the part of her brain that wanted as much time as possible with Beck in the next two days to shut the heck up. He was busy working, who knew how free he'd be or whether he'd even want to spend that free time with her?

"Has Beck asked you out again?"

May jerked her eyes over to Clarissa, methodically laying out seeds. How did she do that? "I haven't heard from him today."

"You will. He had that look about him."

"What look?"

"The look of a man who wants a woman." She gazed pointedly at May, who of course demonstrated her utter unflappability by dropping her eyes and blushing fiercely.

She knew the look of a man who wants a woman. She'd seen that look from Trevor, and once upon a time from Dan. That wasn't the look she wanted from Beck. Well, okay, it was one of them. But she might as well face it, for all her attempts to distance herself from the longings, she wanted those kisses last night to have been inspired by May, not Veronica. And she wanted them to have meant something to him. Whereas she was pretty sure if Trevor had shown up and all had gone according to plan, she never would have cared one way or the other about his.

So now what? Torture herself by going on pretending to be Veronica when she simply wasn't? Risking that the more she fell for Beck, the more he might fall for someone she wasn't? That didn't seem smart at all.

"Did I mention what I like so much about morning glories?"

May glanced at her, startled. Hadn't they just done the morning-glory thing? "I think you might have."

"The thing I like about morning glories is that they only bloom once." She gazed over the lettuce bed, past the peppers and cucumbers to the vines embracing the railing, a tangle of heart-shaped leaves decorated with blue, purple and pink flowers striped with white. "Only for one morning."

"Right." May concentrated on her remaining lettuce seeds to avoid looking concerned. Was Clarissa not as sharp as she first seemed?

"In the jungle, they have to go after what they want, chase all the way up the trees to the sunlight, as fast as they can for their short chance."

"Yes." She patted the last bit of dirt in place and stayed where she was, a little embarrassed and unsure how to handle this.

"So?"

May lifted her head. Clarissa knelt on her black cushion, her floral skirt spread around her the way an artist might arrange it for a portrait. A breeze caught one of her white curls, lifted it, then dropped it gently back into place as if not daring to disturb her coiffure.

"So…I'm sorry, I'm not following."

"It's simple." Clarissa gestured to the vines. "Beck wants you. It's a place to start. Go for the sun as fast as you can in the time you have and see what kind of blooming you can do."

"IT'S BRILLIANT." Alex's shout of delight through the phone line preceded even a hello.

Beck let out a long relieved breath. He'd been up a good part of the night writing the damn scene, slept for a few early hours, then was back at it again, revising chapter after chapter, possessed as he was only at his most inspired, those rare and fabulous moments when words tumbled out of his brain faster than he could keep up with them on the keyboard. Days that made up for the all-too-many others when he needed pliers to extract even a paragraph from his subconscious.

"Thanks, Alex."

"It's exactly what I was after. Exactly the difference I was looking for. It's real, she's real, the scene is hot, oh, my God, I was fanning myself reading it."

"Thanks." The word came out flat. He was happy with the scene himself, and pleasing his agent was always a good thing, but somehow he couldn't get himself excited.

"You even have some tenderness there at the end, when he kissed her, I was like whoa, Mack has a heart? Women are going to fall madly in love with this guy, Beck, and men will only identify more. This is what we want."

"I'm glad." He went to the window, drew back the curtain and frowned at the sheets of water drenching the city. Damn. He'd planned to spend lunch and the afternoon at an outdoor café, recharging his batteries with caffeine and a different setting.

"Now…"

"Yes?" He let the curtain fall and sighed. They always wanted more.

"Now I want more. Through the rest of the book. I want him to fall in love with this woman. You've got a great start here, with Mack feeling these unfamiliar feelings. Now you've got to go the rest of the way, tie that into the plot, the danger, then into the final scene where he has to rescue her. Up the stakes at that point, make it his heart that's at risk of being destroyed, as well as his woman. You got me?"

"Gotcha."

She laughed, that smoky-throated guffaw that alternately amused him and grated on his nerves. "I'm just blown away by this, Beck. What did you do, hire some woman to whack off for you?"

"Jesus, Alex."

"I'm sorry, I'm kidding. But I have to ask, why didn't you ever show me anything like this before?"

Because I didn't know it existed. "I didn't think it fit the character."

"Well it does. It fits the character the way the character should be, Beck, the way readers are going to respond to him and to her in droves. Oh, and you need to come up with a new name for this woman, I don't like Susie after all."

"Thank God."

"What else were you thinking?"

"Off the top of my head?"

"Sure, gut reaction. First two female names you think of."

"April? June?"

"Not May?"

He winced. "No, not May."

"Hmm. I like May. But keep thinking…I've got to take a call, Beck. Love it, love it, love it, you're fabulous. Talk to you later."

Beck punched off his phone. Yeah, he was fabulous, whatever. If last night was any indication, this book was going to kill him. Yes, the words had poured out of him, yes, the adrenaline had been amazing, but afterward, he'd barely been able to sleep, his mind still going a hundred miles an hour, going over the scene, going over the evening, having a few very bizarre tricks of the mind when the two merged into one.

Of course he was writing partly from his own experience; no author could escape who he was. And the deeper you dug into a character, inevitably the deeper you found yourself digging into your own psyche.

But the section where Mack kissed—whatever her name was, not May—had been some of the toughest writing of his career, leaving him drained and feeling exposed and uncomfortable. Maybe this was where his career should go, but writing macho fantasy was a hell of a lot easier.

Now Alex wanted more. She wanted Mack to fall in love the rest of the way.

The problem? Beck wasn't sure he'd ever been in love himself. Or was capable of it. How could he be sure the way he'd portray falling in love would be any less of a fantasy than the dildo scene he'd tried before?

Whenever he got involved with a woman, the same set of rules applied. He was attracted, turned on the confidence, the charm, the women fell, he enjoyed them, lusted, was mildly infatuated for a while and then things quieted down to a nice level of comfortable companionship that suited him fine and caused the women no end of aggravation and resentment, and eventually they broke it off.

Frankly, by that time he'd usually grown so tired of hearing how he was lacking as a romantic partner, he was glad to be free again. Until he met the next one and it all played out again. No relationship and no woman had ever consumed him the way he imagined readers wanted to read about. The way the romance novels he'd read on a girlfriend's recommendation portrayed it.

He'd made peace with that. Until…the encounters he'd had so far with May broke all the patterns he'd gotten so used to they barely made an impression anymore. What made her so different? He enjoyed her, he lusted, same as usual, but last night he'd experienced something he'd never felt before with a woman. Vulnerability. Anxiety. Even a sense of sadness when he looked ahead to her leaving Friday.

When he'd been writing, he found himself putting into Mack's head thoughts he was dimly aware were too terrifying to acknowledge in his own.

Now what? He'd told May he'd see her today. He wanted to see her…and he didn't. He had an instinctive feeling that if last night was anything to go by, he would not be able to glide through a relationship with her in control of himself and his emotions. Was this what he had to do to understand what Mack would be going through? Did this mean *he* was going to fall in love?

He ran his hands down his face, gritty with stubble. It wasn't like him to be so melodramatic. Lack of sleep and the passionate intensity with which he'd attacked his scene last night must have colored his view. May was a beautiful woman. One he was beginning to suspect had more to her than his original impression of a Sugar-daddy girl. Maybe it was just the twin images of siren and sweet that had him confused and off balance.

In two days he could hardly be on the path to love that Mack was supposed to travel. He needed to separate the two in his mind. One had most likely informed the other.

His room phone rang and he lunged for it, hoping like hell it was her.

"Mr. Desmond? I'm sorry to bother you, there's a Jeffrey Desmond here in the lobby. He says he's your brother."

"Yes." He stood abruptly. What the hell was Jeffrey doing here? "Send him up."

He changed his shirt, wishing he had time to shower, pulled the covers up and straightened a few piles of paper, not that his brother would care. But if it got back to Mom that he lived and looked like an exhausted slob, she'd worry more than she did already.

His brother knocked on the door and Beck let him in, grinning in welcome. He and Jeffrey had next to nothing in common, but what they did have was shared blood and a shared childhood, and that counted for a lot.

"Hey, Beck, you look like hell, what's going on? You

seen the sun this year at all?" Jeffrey was bursting with vitality, the tallest, darkest and handsomest of the three brothers, he was also a loyal, lovable, self-centered pain in the ass. "Whoa, nice digs."

"I was up all night writing."

Jeffrey frowned and shook his head. "No, you got it wrong there, guy. At your age, up all night should involve women, preferably twins."

Beck thought of May and suppressed a smile. "Yeah, I guess I'll never be in your league, stud. What brings you? Mom send you to guilt me into going to your birthday party Thursday?"

Jeffrey laughed. "Actually, no. I wanted to tell you I'm getting engaged."

"Wow, no kidding." Beck extended his hand, then pulled him in for a manly backslap, trying not to show his surprise. Jeffrey was a legendary love-'em-and-leave-'em commitment phobe. "Who's the lucky woman."

"Remember Mary Costanzas?"

"Mary?" He remembered all right. A tiny thing, with the biggest mouth in the neighborhood and a heart sized to match. "Is she old enough to date?"

Jeffrey rolled his eyes. "You've been in this room too long, man."

"I'm kidding. I'm happy for you."

"I am, too." His eyes softened. "She's something else. She graduated from college in Jersey in May, comes into the restaurant one night last month, walks back into the kitchen to see me, I look up from my veal cutlets and bang, I'm gone."

"Just like that?" Two days with May and what had Beck told himself minutes ago about how—

"That's all it took me, professor. You'd probably need to analyze it and write about it for a few months first."

Beck chuckled dryly. Touché. Though he'd give his method better odds of long-term success. "Yeah, that's me. But I'm not the one who shoved his head between the planks of Mrs. Polansky's back fence trying to see up her skirt and got stuck."

"Very true. Caution isn't always a bad thing." Jeffrey backed to the door. "I can't stay, I just wanted to tell you in person about Mary and me in case you can't make it Thursday. I was actually on my way to the library to meet her and I look over, boom, here you are in your fancy sex palace. Though if you ask me, the only difference between this place and the Easy Come Easy Go Motel is the price."

Beck laughed. His brother had a brilliant way of distilling the world into its essential elements.

"Tell Mom I'll try to be there Thursday." He held the door open. "I'd like to see Mary again, and be there for your official announcement. I'm just not sure—"

"I know, I know. You have to doodle your stories."

Beck shook his head in exasperation. "Something like that."

"Hey, we're proud of what you do." Jeffrey slapped him on the back. "We think you're some kind of serious freak, but we're all proud. Even Dad."

"Thanks." He grinned, touched in spite of himself. "I think."

"See you Thursday, maybe."

A stunning female uniformed member of housekeeping walked by in the hall behind Jeffrey, and smiled alluringly at Beck. "Good morning, Mr. Desmond."

"Good morning."

Jeffrey watched her rear undulate down the hall.

"Whoa. You duh man here, huh? Why don't you bring a date on Thursday? We're all starting to think you're turning queer."

Beck sighed and banished the image of May bewildered by his overwhelming family. "Not queer, just working too hard. But that will be over on Friday. For a while at least."

"Cool. Well if you can't come Thursday, stop by the restaurant over the weekend. Mary's helping out to give Mom a day or two off."

"Sounds good." He said goodbye to his brother, got an awkward hug and closed the door. He hadn't been back to the restaurant for a while, and for a second he missed it retroactively. The cheesy, cheery comfortable decor, the noxious music, the overwhelming portions of good honest food. People loved the place, had loved it for over a generation.

At the same time, Jeffrey's visit had only underscored how uncomfortable he felt with his own family, how different he was not only in coloring—he took after his father's sister—but in temperament. He brought up a mental picture of May's quiet sophistication—like he'd been thinking of much else for the past two days?—and felt even more drawn to her.

More than that, after his brother's drive-by visit, Beck's reasons for avoiding her pull were suddenly and thoroughly exposed as cowardly and unconvincing, especially seen through Jeffrey's testosterone-guided eyes. If Jeff could fall in love with a glance, at very least Beck could go for a second date.

And didn't that make him sound like a wild player.

8

Note on Exhibit A waitstaff board:

Beck Desmond is going to be at Exhibit A tonight. Ladies, I know he's tempting but I want good behavior all around.
Frank

Note scrawled on bottom:

When we're good, we're good. When we're bad, we're better!

A LITTLE APPREHENSIVE May descended to the basement level of HUSH. Beck's invitation to meet at a room called Exhibit A had come in a phone call after her postlunch swim and before an indulgent afternoon nap. They'd chatted briefly and, to her disappointment, impersonally. After last night, she'd hoped for something more. But he was probably in the middle of working, and what did she expect anyway, heavy breathing? At least during the call she'd managed to keep her voice cheerful and had accepted his invitation with a combination of thrill and relief.

Thrill because she'd see him again. Relief because…she'd see him again. And get another chance to figure out what she was feeling. She'd decided during her swim that Clarissa and her morning glories had a point. She'd play down Veronica tonight. Give Beck the real May and see how he reacted. If all went well, then…

Hang on, May. One minute at a time. She needed to enjoy being with him tonight and stop the whole what-about-tomorrow anxiety.

The elevator doors opened; she stepped out into a low-ceilinged white narrow hallway. A sign had been painted on the wall opposite her, black lettering and an arrow pointing left: Exhibit A.

What was this place? Why did he want to meet here? He'd mumbled something about more research, but he couldn't possibly expect her to repeat last night's performance in public. Even the hotel literature was vague on the subject. Something about low lights and privacy and tasteful live entertainment. Of course if the couple in the hot tub was anything to go by, there seemed to be plenty of live entertainment happening all over.

Twenty yards on the left, a doorway painted black, with a white sign, Exhibit A. May put her hand to the door. Music sounded faintly inside, an anemic female vocal over a pulsing beat. She didn't love going into places she couldn't see into. And she didn't love that no one else was around.

But if Beck was in there, she'd do it.

She tentatively pushed the swinging door; it gave easily. Her first impressions: cool air, semidarkness, dim blue lights that cast an eerie glow and smoke. Lots of smoke. She grimaced, anticipating a choking ciga-rette smell at the same time her senses registered none. The "smoke" probably came from a fog machine like the one her high school drama department had rented when they'd put on *Brigadoon*.

Banquettes and tables facing center lined the walls and filled the room, some empty, some inhabited. She squinted through the blue cavelike gloom for Beck and came up empty. The music enveloped her, the crooning voice, words she couldn't understand, and under it that insistent beat keeping time with her thudding heart.

In the middle of the room, a stage—a platform, really—spotlit with a smoky white-blue glare. On the platform, a man and a woman, short hair slicked back, faces impassive, two perfect bodies each wearing a G-string…and nothing else. They posed facing each other, the woman lunging to the right, the man to his left, their arms encircling each other, mimicking caresses without touching anywhere. May watched, the thump of music in her chest, while the man's broad hands stroked a path through the air over the woman's body where a lover's touch would travel. The sight was beautiful and erotic, weird and entrancing at the same time.

But where was Beck?

The instant she had the thought, she saw him. He was making his way toward her, smiling that smile that made her energy and spirits rise like a hot-air balloon. Someone should market the man as an antidepressant.

"Hello, May." Even lit a ghostly blue, he still managed to look wildly sexy and her heart shifted away from the music's beat to launch into a skittering solo. She smiled back, hoping the blue look suited her equally. He took her hand and led her toward his table; she followed, watching his hair glisten blue-blond then blue-brown as he traveled in and out of the light.

They reached his banquette and table; the curving

high sides would hide them from parties on the left and right, but permitted a full view of the stage. The high cloth-covered table gave a further sense of privacy from the spread of the room in front of them, and gave May a pretty good idea what the room was for.

Sex in semipublic? Exhibit A as in exhibitionism? She braced herself for panic and found herself more excited than anxious. Had Veronica come along tonight after all? Maybe it hadn't sunk in yet. Or maybe the hotel had temporarily transformed her.

Maybe everything felt right when she was with Beck.

She slid along the couch, not caring that her yellow miniskirt with the double rows of pleats at the hem slid up her leg. She'd been tempted to wear something more demure to go with her more discreet makeup application, something more like the real her, like the skirt from her traveling suit. In the end, she couldn't bring herself to look that plain, and settled on this yellow number instead, and an off-shoulder white knit top with a double layer of fabric over her breasts that was supposed to function as a built-in bra. On her way out of the room, she'd stopped impulsively and kicked off her panties, then left quickly before she changed her mind.

At the time she figured no one but her would know. In her persona as May she was unlikely to end up in Beck's room unless he seemed serious about a relationship with her.

But now…tonight…here, in this exciting atmosphere…maybe she'd get to share her secret with Beck right here, which would make it less secret but ten times more exciting. And why wasn't she freaking?

"You look beautiful. But then you always do."

May smiled, loving the compliment, wanting to tell him that he made her feel beautiful just by being with him.

So maybe she should. Besides, she'd promised herself all-May, all the time. "You make me feel beautiful."

Instead of beaming and complimenting her further, his eyes narrowed. "Is that a new experience for you?"

A flicker of surprise revealed that Dan criticized her appearance more than he praised it. Funny how easy it was to get so used to behavior that you didn't notice it anymore. They'd been together such a long time—when had she stopped noticing?

"Hi, I'm Jessie, I'll be serving you this evening. Can I get you a drink?" A stunning dark-haired leggy waitress in a blue and white swirling patterned minidress stood perfectly poised, full lips puckered, eyes devouring Beck.

Grrrreow. May slipped out of one yellow high heel, which frankly, was ridiculously uncomfortable, and hooked her foot around Beck's calf, reached and drew a languid finger down the short hair at the nape of his neck. "What do you feel like drinking?"

She almost called him darling, but didn't want to push her luck.

Beck turned amused blue-gray eyes to her that nearly took her breath away, as they did practically every time he looked at her. If they were together a long time would she stop noticing, the way she had with Dan?

"Ever had a mojito?"

A mo-hee-what? Veronica would have had millions. But she wasn't Veronica tonight. "Never."

"Two mojitos." He didn't take his eyes off May, which suited her fine. Jessie nodded and undulated away, defeat accepted graciously.

"A mojito?" She took her arm back from behind him. Catty point made, it seemed too forward to be touching him, though her fingers desperately wanted to go exploring. "What did I just get myself into?"

"Rum, mint and lime."

"Hmm, sounds dangerous." Veronica's throaty voice came out of her mouth and May blinked. Where had she come from?

"It can be." He slid a finger from her knee down to her bare toe. Any other man could touch her like that and she'd smile politely. Beck's finger made her pretty sure her shin had a G-spot. "That's the fun of it."

"Mmm, I think I'll like that kind of fun." More Veronica. What was she doing? She pitched her voice higher and sat up straighter. "You've never been down here before?"

"No. I've explored most of the rest of the hotel by myself. This place seemed better with company." Again that smile that brightened her universe. "I'm glad I met you."

He said the words casually enough, but watched her carefully, which made her nervous. How to respond? Glibly? Carefully? In a you're-my-best-buddy manner?

"I'm glad, too." To her horror her voice came out thick with emotion. Please, God, let the music in the room be loud enough to camouflage the evidence of her inane infatuation.

If she revealed that much May all at once he'd run screaming out into the night. Desperately needing a change of subject, she gestured toward the models, then did a double take. They'd moved—maybe they were still moving?—but with the perfect control of dancers, until the woman stood straight, arms and face reaching for the ceiling, back arched slightly. The man had bent forward, his face an inch from her right breast, lips parted as if an invisible wall was keeping him from his goal.

The woman's eyes closed, the glitter in her exotic heavy eye shadow caught the bright light, her dark hair gleamed, her chest rose and fell in the exaggerated breathing of arousal, bringing her nipple close to the man's reaching lips, then away, then back. The music swelled, then settled into a steady, hot rhythm.

May arched her chest forward before she realized what she was doing. She wanted to see the man's lips close over the skin of the small perfect breast, wanted to see the woman's impassive expression melt into pleasure.

What had this hotel done to her?

"Look at them." Beck's voice was close to her ear. "Very sexy."

His scent reached her and May did a little melting into pleasure of her own. She wanted to turn and offer him her mouth, plow her fingers through his cool spiky hair, pull his head to her breast to give her what the woman on stage was being denied.

"Yes. It's…lovely." Lovely? Hot, sensual, arousing.

"If someone described this place, I wouldn't have thought 'lovely.'"

"No." She looked away from the posing couple, drawn by Beck's voice. Again, she took a dive into those fabulous eyes and realized what people meant by drowning in someone's gaze. What was it about him that affected her so powerfully? Lust? Atmosphere? Did it have more to do with who she wanted to be or who he was? Right now, with the pulsing beat, the dim lights and the skillful illusion of privacy at their table, she didn't care. The now-familiar thrill, the desire to be daring pushed at her again.

He gazed down at her mouth and the gaze hit her like a kiss—her lips tingled; her nipples pushed out the stretchy fabric of her top, which drew his eyes down and spread the tingling farther.

She wanted him. Right here, right now, in front of everyone. What the hell was the matter with her?

"Here you go." Jessie served them two tall cloudy drinks with lime wedges in the bottom and mint leaves floating on the surface, bringing May back from her absurd need to be naked every time Beck was within two feet of her.

"Here's to Hush."

May clinked her glass with Beck's and took her first sip of the tangy, minty, slightly sweet liquid—an admittedly large sip. "Delicious."

He fished a mint leaf out of his drink, leaned over and tickled it over her lips, then fed her. She accepted the offering, letting her tongue brush over his fingers, wanting to draw one in and suck. Instead, she straightened so his hand lost contact. He pulled it back. "I discovered mojitos on a trip to Miami one year."

"Do you travel a lot?" She congratulated herself. *Do you travel a lot?* had nothing to do with sex.

"A fair amount. This is the first book I've set in my home city. You can't describe any place as well as the one you live in." He took another mint leaf, used it as a brush to paint her lips with rum and lime, then let her capture it between her teeth. "As they say, 'Write what you know.'"

"Yes, I've heard that." She was dying. On fire. She wanted him to touch her again, again and again, absolutely everywhere. "Why haven't you used New York before this?"

Her question seemed to take him aback, which meant he didn't dip into rum for the next mint leaf, which meant he didn't reach to touch her again, which meant she was immensely disappointed. "I'm not sure. Maybe because I live here, it didn't feel that exotic to me. Not much of a fantasy place."

"So this book is more real to you?"

He stopped with his drink pressed against his amazingly sexy mouth, then pulled it down and held the glass with both hands between his knees. "I hadn't thought about it like that. Maybe…it will end up that way."

She nodded politely, but he'd said the last sentence slowly, looking at her as if he'd never seen her before, and something about the intensity in his eyes caused a mass butterfly migration in her stomach. Why would this book end up more real? Did that have something to do with her?

"Have *you* done a lot of traveling?" He asked in a polite conversational tone and May wished like mad they were back to mint leaf art.

"Oh…" Hesitation she couldn't quite control ambushed her; she was so used to hiding May—or so ashamed of her—she couldn't let herself out without an effort. "No. Not really. I'd like to do more."

"Where would you like to go?"

Where wouldn't she? "Paris, for a start."

"City of lovers."

"Yes." She sipped her mojito, searching frantically for some other topic, to stop herself thinking how much she wanted him to say he'd take her there next week.

The music changed to a more sultry beat. Fresh smoke blew in and swirled blue-white around the models. The woman executed a slow, controlled back-bend until she had one hand on the floor, the other raised high, head hanging down. Her partner supported her, one arm at the small of her back, his other raised to the ceiling. For a few moments it seemed they were holding still. May gripped her glass, hardly breathing, trying to control her anticipation. Beside her, Beck didn't move. The whole bar seemed to freeze, waiting for what would happen next.

Slowly, almost imperceptibly, the man moved his pelvis forward, toward the juncture of his partner's spread legs. The spotlight shifted, grew brighter, then dimmed blue; the musical beat quickened.

May took in a slow breath, watching the progress of his barely covered sex toward the soft vee of hers, feeling slightly dizzy. She took a long swallow of her drink and put it on the table, fighting an urge to slide her hand along Beck's thigh, explore his lap and see if he was enjoying the show as much as she was.

The music grew louder; the lights dimmed farther, the model's impressively bulging groin made contact with the tiny strip of white material covering his partner's sex. Oh—oh—oh. May tilted her pelvis up, pushing against an imaginary male. The dark yearning grew inside her. Why hadn't she ever felt this way before with Dan? Except maybe right before her peak, when this same type of wildness sometimes took her over.

Beck's fingers made contact with her bare knee at the same time hers made contact with his linen-covered one and Dan was totally forgotten. She moved back against the couch, let her knees fall open, fairly sure the table hid her from the waitresses and patrons walking about, but not caring as much as May ought to. "Is this what you brought me here for?"

His hand moved up her thigh at the same slow pace hers moved up his. "Not entirely."

"Oh?" She was whispering, aching for his hand to complete the journey.

"I'm revising a scene. Exhibit A seemed like a promising place for a new idea."

"What idea?"

"The usual." He was whispering, too, and his breath seemed to be coming faster than normal. "Seemed like a good place to kill someone."

May winced. "You're not going to want me to try *that,* are you?"

"No." He let his eyes wander down the length of her exposed thigh, which made her want to open her legs and let him see what she wasn't wearing. "But being down here with you has given me some other ideas, too."

"Really." She blinked sweetly. "About murder?"

"Not exactly."

"Suicide?"

"No."

"A tasteful maiming?"

"Much less violent."

"Tell me."

"I'd rather show you."

"Show me." She whispered the words and managed to shock herself with how hot and desperate she sounded. She was out of her mind already. He or the hotel or something had her in some kind of sexual spell. Or maybe she'd pretended to be Veronica for so long she couldn't go back. She'd be stuck like this forever. Walk into work Monday morning and immediately try to seduce half the campus.

The thought of going back to the office seemed so

barren and dull and horrible that she pushed the thought as far away as possible and concentrated on Beck, who instead of starting something hot immediately, leaned forward, hand still on her thigh, took a small card on the table, and propped it against his drink.

"What's that?"

He turned back and gave her a wicked grin. "Do not disturb."

"Oh, I like that."

"So do I."

The music slowed. The male model began a gentle rocking, undulating his body against the woman in time to the newly relaxed beat.

May settled herself against the hard muscle of Beck's side, letting the arousal build, sliding her hand slowly the rest of the way up his thigh, feeling his warm hand sliding slowly the rest of the way up hers.

She was wet already; she strained for his touch where she needed it most. As arousing as it had been lying on his bed fantasizing about him, this was ten times more so. Enticing, erotic, daring, dangerous. May would never do anything like this. And here she was, wanting to do it all.

The blue light changed to a frantic strobe, flashing around the room, framing reality in brief snapshot bursts. She found his hardness; his fingers found her, and she released a small "oh" of blissful relief.

He groaned, and his penis surged against her hand. "You're not wearing panties."

"No."

"You just about killed me." His voice was low next to her ear; she drew back so their lips were inches apart, the strobe flash making the visual strange and untrustworthy. Only the touch was real, and he felt hard and large and real against her hand.

"There's your murder scene." She murmured the words, stopped for a breath as his fingers parted her and explored. "Death by no panties."

"Ah, but they'd die happy."

Their waitress, Jessie, walked by close to their table; May tensed, closing her knees reflexively.

"Relax. They're trained not to look." His low whisper brushed her hair. "I wanted to touch you like this so badly when you were on my bed."

"Why didn't you?" She stroked him through his pants and felt him lengthen, harden, strain against the fabric. She wanted him out.

"Because you were so good on your own." He found her clitoris, started a rhythm like the one she used herself—he knew how to please her exactly the way she liked it best, because she'd been able to show him.

She fumbled with his fly, praying she could please him half that well. Pants unzipped, she put in exploring fingers and found he'd worn as much underwear as she had. The hard male heat felt so perfect, so smooth, so inviting. For a second she wished they were in a room, his or hers, on a big bed, so she could taste him, take him inside her. In the next second she was grateful they weren't. How far and fast would she fall for him if she allowed him that close? Women like May couldn't handle intense sex and then goodbye. It was better this way, public and controlled.

She matched his stroking rhythm; the couple on the stage sped theirs in time to the frantic beat of the music and the strobe. The man's body thrust harder, lifting his partner with each push, then letting her back down, his body undulating in earnest, sweat glistening on his torso.

May spread her legs wider, kicked off her other shoe and pressed her feet together, any desire to be private or discreet lost to the passion and arousal in and around her. Beck's fingers dipped into her in time to the music, smoke swirled, the couple gyrated in a mock sex dance. Her hand closed over the top of Beck's penis; she felt drops of liquid and used them to lubricate the motion, loving that his body tensed next to her, and his fingers grew momentarily clumsy.

The music blared, filled the bar, made conversation impossible; the couple's motions became less dancerly, more animal. May turned from the sight, wanting to watch Beck, wanting to experience his pleasure, to share hers with him. He met her eyes and suddenly the crazy give-and-take flash of the strobe, the feel of his cock in her hand, the plunge of his fingers inside her, and most of all, the hot look in his eyes, made the need to come overwhelm her.

His name came to her lips and she lunged for his mouth, joined hers to his in a frenzy of kissing that sent her over the edge in a stomach-tightening free fall. She moaned in his mouth and moments later felt his moisture on her hand, warm drops of his pleasure that prolonged hers for the deep and unexpected joy of sharing ecstasy.

This was the way it should be. This was—

This was sex in public. And she was falling for him, like the impressionable easily dazzled vulnerable small-town girl she was.

The noise and strobe light in the bar became disorienting, claustrophobic. A sudden pressure in her chest signaled tears on the way up. No. Bad. Wrong.

She tried to smile sexily into his eyes, but had a feeling she was gazing adoringly at him instead, which wasn't the plan at all. Worse than sobbing.

Oh, no. Please don't let her ruin this by being May now. The evening had been so perfect the way it was, even if she had been more Veronica than herself. All she needed to ruin everything was this desperate vulnerable need to know if he felt the deep overwhelming feelings she felt.

"May." He kissed her gently, savoring her lips as if they were the sweetest treat he'd ever tasted. He drew back and the strobe slowed, stopped; the music quieted. "You amaze me. Or maybe *we* amaze me."

"We?"

Of course she tried not to look hopeful. Of course she failed. And of course instead of saying, "Yes, you are obviously the love of my life," Beck just looked uncertain, and began getting himself cleaned up, put away and zipped, which was necessary, but not romantic.

Time to back off. "You mean the fact that we nearly melted the couch?"

"Yes." His face relaxed into a smile. "I'm not sure I've ever experienced this much…melting power before."

"Oh?" *Oh?* Because she sure as hell hadn't, either. So maybe she wasn't alone in this? Maybe she should stop being such a chicken and risk admitting how she felt. "I haven't, either. This is really…special."

He nodded, gave a small smile and reached for his drink. May felt like dropping her forehead onto her hand and groaning. Oh, for Pete's sake. They'd just given each other hand jobs in public and she was calling it special?

Except…it had been. The arousal in her body had triggered something much deeper in her heart, regardless of the less than classically romantic circumstances. But based on what? They'd barely had more than a couple of conversations. Strong sexual attraction wasn't exactly a solid foundation for a relationship.

Even though, yes, it was a hell of a fun place to start.

She and Dan had—used to have—much more than this. Tastes in common. Shared friends, habits, values. What did she know about Beck except that he turned her on? She needed to back away from this overpowering emotion before she opened her mouth and blurted out something idiotically premature. "Special" was bad enough.

"So. How is the romanticizing of Mack going?" Her voice came out too high, too chipper, and the question seemed grossly out of place.

Beck shot her a look, acknowledging her need to change the subject, though she couldn't tell if he was grateful or not. "The scene you helped me with went like gangbusters. My agent loved it, she called today and said my editor loved it, too."

"Oh, good." She smiled, absurdly pleased. "I'm glad I could help."

"Me, too." He drained his drink and put the glass down. Silence settled over their table.

"Just think." She gave a stupid-sounding laugh. "In a way, millions of readers will be watching me touch myself. Funny."

He nodded in a distant way, watching the now-empty stage as if there was something still there to see. Was he trying to think of a way to extract himself from the evening? Maybe she should finish her drink and make the first move.

She was about to reach for her glass, when he took her hand and held it loosely, stroking her fingers with his thumb, which didn't seem like something a man trying to extract himself would do. Oh, that was nice. She could sit here and hold hands with this man all day, not that she minded being blown out of her mind by orgasms, either.

"How's the rest of the book going?" Her voice came out dreamy and contented this time, and the question seemed natural and just right.

"I'm not sure yet."

"Why not?"

He lifted her hand to his lips and kissed each finger, slow, deliberate kisses that nearly made her slide off the couch. "Mack has to fall in love."

"And?" Ohhhhh, if he didn't stop being so fabulously romantic she was going to fall more in love than Mack could ever hope to. Until this moment she thought the whole hand-kissing routine was fake and overblown. But Beck Desmond made it seem genuine and sexy and…well, loving. She dared hope.

"Write what you know." He lowered her hand, gave it a gentle squeeze. "Mack's never fallen in love. And I'm…starting to think I haven't, either."

"Starting to think?"

Argh! Why did she say that out loud? She could cheerfully strangle herself, except that it wasn't physically possible. What now, blink yearningly at him until things got so awkward neither of them could stand it?

A corner of his mouth lifted in a grin, sadly on the non-dimple side. "Maybe Mack…and I…have just been with the wrong women."

Oh—oh—oh. Was the fake smoke in the bar making it hard to breathe? Or had her heart just stopped? Was he really saying what she so wanted him to be saying?

Except…for one problem.

There was always a problem.

Until tonight, she'd been posing as someone else. Even tonight, for all her vows to the contrary, she hadn't exactly done much to show him the farm girl she really was. He knew next to nothing about her. Any feelings he might be developing…if he was…were as far out in fantasy as one of his books.

And yet…she was enough of a Pollyanna optimist…

"Maybe Mack has been with women that are too perfect, too New York, too sexual. Maybe he needs someone who is a total contrast to him. Like a nice girl from…the country. Maybe from…" She gestured aimlessly, while her brain instructed her not to say Wisconsin. "…Iowa."

Beck frowned.

May held her breath.

"Maybe."

Maybe. That was good. Better than, *no way in hell*. "Maybe someone with an unglamorous office job, not worldly, not sophisticated, but honest and supportive and…"

God she sounded dull.

"Hmm." He rubbed his chin back and forth on his thumb. "Nice idea. But I can't see a woman like that holding Mack's interest for more than a chapter or two."

Fwoosh. May's precious little fantasy went up in flames. She couldn't hold Mack's interest. And therefore not Beck's. *Write what you know*.

How naive could she be? Apparently very. She took a long swallow of her drink and put it down a little harder on the table than she needed to. Well that was just clucking ducky, as her mom would say.

Enough. She was drained, and wanted out of this weird noisy kinky place. She didn't belong here. "So are you done with your research?"

"I'm sorry?"

"Did you accomplish what you wanted to?" She gestured between them. "Professionally?"

He shook his head slightly, frowning. "That's not what I was doing."

"But you said—"

"That's not what this is about, May."

"Then what is it about?"

He looked perplexed and she would have shut herself up except she was too hurt to care. "I don't know. But it's about a lot more than research. And a lot more than...couch melting."

"Oh?" She knew exactly why. Because the woman she'd showed him was about a hundred times more exciting than she was. The thrill every man wanted times ten. She just had nothing to do with May.

He took hold of her shoulders, brought her close and kissed her eyes, her temples and finally her mouth, then leaned his forehead against hers. "I want to see as much as possible of you, May. I wish you were going to be here a hell of a lot longer than just one week, because I've never felt this way about anyone, and certainly not in three days."

There. There it was, all of it. Everything she felt about him, everything she wanted to say, reflected back at her as she'd dreamed.

Just one little problem.

9

Note on Exhibit A waitstaff board:

Hey, Jessie, I'm happy to take your shift tonight at Exhibit A. Think Beck will be there again? Maybe I'll have more luck seducing him away from his new love than you did, ha!
Ciao
Sarah

Note on Exhibit A waitstaff board:

Thank you, Sarah!!!! You're a goddess. Yeah, good luck with Beck. He only had eyes for Ms. Ellison! Bet housekeeping only had to change one pair of sheets for them this morning!
Jess

"TAXI, MA'AM?"

May smiled at today's hunky doorman, shook her head and thanked him. No taxi. In one hand she clutched bus directions to Clarissa's apartment. In the other, she held a bag containing her sketch pad and drawings. Maybe Clarissa was just being polite, but she seemed sincere about wanting to see the drawings when she called to confirm their tea date this afternoon, so May brought them.

This morning, after opening Trevor's daily gift—bright orange fur-trimmed lingerie, oh thankyouverymuch—she'd decided not to return Ginny's call and had gone for a swim instead. The situation with Beck was complicated, May's feelings were complicated, and she wasn't in the mood for Ginny's over-the-top romantic interpretations or advice.

After her swim, she'd gone up to the roof garden to touch up some of the sketches she'd done the previous day, to use her new pencils to add color and life. Up there the humidity had lightened, the temperature had dropped, the sky had been a shade of blue deeper than any she'd seen in Wisconsin, clouds a dazzling white contrast, foliage in the garden vibrant green and lush.

Even the surrounding buildings seemed cleaner, less angular, somehow they blended in better with the landscape. Maybe she was getting used to the idea of nature existing midair amid concrete like this. Maybe that's what New Yorkers did: grabbed a slice of green wherever they could get it and hung on for dear life.

She'd also ventured out this morning to a shop the concierge recommended and had found a cotton flowered dress, flattering and pretty without being revealing or trampy. The clothes in her suitcase were suitable for a week of hay-rolling in a sex palace, nothing that would cut it for afternoon tea with a lady as elegant as Clarissa—except the damn traveling suit, and that seemed more like a straitjacket these days.

Heading over to Fifth Avenue, she let her arms swing, going with the crowds, acting more confident than she felt, but feeling pretty good. It helped to have a concrete destination and a surefire way of getting there.

The bus stop appeared just where Clarissa said it would on the corner of West 42nd Street and Fifth. May waited with a harried-looking mother of twin toddlers until the M5 appeared.

After helping the grateful mom with her boys and bags, May chose a seat next to an older woman, instead of the teenage boy with so many body parts pierced he looked mechanical, and sat back in relief. First stage accomplished.

The bus moved on, traveling slowly south on Fifth Avenue, stop after stop, letting teenagers and business people and families, couples and seniors on and off. The mom with twin toddlers disembarked near Broadway, and a few people helped her with her stroller and packages after one of her boys sat down in the aisle of the bus and refused to move. The driver chuckled and made a remark about being glad his own kids were grown, which made several passengers smile and nod.

A different view of the city entirely.

Then it was May's turn to press the Stop Requested strip, feeling like a pro commuter. The driver stopped, obligingly, and she stepped off, admiring the beautifully maintained yellow brick apartments, taking in the people strolling about holding cups of coffee and copies of the *New York Times*, and walking their dogs. For all its luxury and promise and excitement, HUSH receded as the fantasy it was. This was part of the real New York, a glimpse of people living regular lives. The city felt so different from this perspective. Energizing, not deadening, manageable, not overwhelming. She could see why her mother had come and why she'd stayed.

And why had she gone back?

May stopped on the sidewalk, staring at Washington Square Park ahead of her, at the triumphal arch, which defined the park. Her own life in Wisconsin would be a huge comedown after this trip; it was only starting to sink in how tough the transition would be, even apart from leaving Beck and whatever they were starting. Yes, also something of a relief—day after day of new experiences was draining—but for the first time, May could see the weeks and years of her life back home stretching ahead of her, without feeling the old feelings of safety and contentment. More like the claustrophobia she felt when she first arrived here.

Her hand went to the place on her chest where Dan's grandmother's locket used to lie. Was this low-level panic what Dan had felt? This resistance to forced confinement in the box of the always-expected? Was it really May that had bored him, or just the rut they'd gotten into as a couple? Was she wrong to have thought life couldn't be more exciting than the one she'd planned for them for so long? That it couldn't at least involve thrills now and then greater than rearranging her furniture?

Beck seemed to think it could. And she'd certainly experienced more thrills at his hands than any others she'd ever encountered, figuratively and literally. Maybe this was all happening for a reason. Maybe she was evolving somehow, maybe this trip was changing her, so she could go back to Wisconsin and drum up a little more excitement. Maybe even get Dan back…

Her cheeks started hurting and she tuned into the giant scowl on her face, forced it to relax and kept walking until she reached Waverly Place. Even assuming Dan's fling would be over soon, could she go back to him now? After what she'd been through here? After what she'd felt for Beck in such a short time? Would she always wonder how far these feelings could have gone? Would that wondering about Beck poison any chance of her and Dan picking up where they'd left off and impede their ability to move forward?

Last night she'd stayed at Exhibit A long enough to make her departure not obviously hasty. She'd both dreaded an invitation to Beck's room and been desperately hoping for one, so when none came, she managed to contort herself emotionally into feeling relieved and miserable at the same time. That was May. Never waste an opportunity to cram as much angst as possible into any given situation. Maybe this was why she liked her life calm and smooth; she seemed to freak at every ripple.

She'd avoided her room today; Beck would have to work for one thing, and she wanted to enjoy herself, not sit scared he'd call and scared he wouldn't. But when she went back to her room to change for tea, she'd found a message from him, asking to meet her that night. She hadn't answered yet; there would be time when she got back.

Quite honestly, she hadn't made up her mind whether to go or how to handle herself if she did. Her feelings were too tangled, her heart too vulnerable and confused to risk it…and yet, his pull was undeniable. Which was why this peaceful time with Clarissa this afternoon would be a godsend.

She reached the entrance to Clarissa's apartment, entered the spotless chandeliered lobby and gave her name to the doorman, who called up and announced her to "Mrs. Armstrong."

"4B." He directed her to the elevator, down a carpeted cream corridor hung with impressionist prints. She pressed the appropriate button and rode the creaky antique up to the fourth floor, where the door to Clarissa's apartment stood open and an enticing smell of cinnamon beckoned.

"Hello, May. I'm so glad you came." Clarissa welcomed her into a spotless foyer, lined cheeks pink, blue eyes warm, lemon-yellow dress blooming with honeysuckle and ivy. "How pretty you look. I like your makeup lighter like that."

"Thank you." May smiled, thinking of Beck, wondering if he'd like her more natural look or wish she was still Veronica'd up.

"Come in."

Clarissa's apartment was large, sunny and high-ceilinged, which May gathered in New York meant serious dollars worth of real estate, and decorated exquisitely— a clawfoot dark wood coffee table, a glass-doored bookshelf with a carved likeness of William Shakespeare on top, African masks, Balinese dragon statues, goddesses from Thailand, and plants everywhere. African violets, ficus trees, bonsai, cyclamen…

"What a beautiful apartment."

"Thank you. Jim and I traveled quite a bit and bought what we liked where we found it. Can't say there's much of an official decorating scheme. Maybe as you like it."

"I do like it."

"Come sit down, I've just put the tea in to steep, it will be ready in a minute."

"Thank you." May sat on a dainty-looking chair that felt sturdy and comfortable under her. Clarissa bustled back and forth from what must be the kitchen, bringing out more food than May could eat in a day. Tea sandwiches and cookies, salted almonds and strawberries, scones and jams and honey and a bowl of what looked like clotted cream.

"Clarissa, this is heaven on earth, you shouldn't have gone to all this trouble."

"Oh, I didn't. Truly. There's the most wonderful bakery and sandwich shop around the corner. I did bake the scones, but even they came from a mix. In New York there's never any excuse to eat poorly, and always an excuse to stay out of the kitchen if you want to."

May thought of the assorted fast-food chains littering the commercial street nearest her in Oshkosh and felt a pang of envy.

Finally, Clarissa brought out the tea service, white china with tiny red roses rambling on leafy green vines, around the teapot and the rims of the cups and saucers.

"You've brought your sketches, thank you." Clarissa lifted the lid of the teapot and stirred. "May I see?"

May nodded and took her drawings out of the bag, wishing she'd left them at home. In a house like this, with art probably worth millions of dollars, her silly amateur scribbling would be an embarrassment, though doubtless Clarissa would gush and exclaim as if May were a genius.

"One minute." Clarissa retrieved a pair of reading glasses from a cherry writing desk and returned to her seat on the deep rose-colored Queen Anne sofa. "Now."

She held the sketches at arm's length, studying them carefully, from the hurried slashing pencil sketch of the garden on May's first day, to the more carefully drawn color study with the hawk she'd finished that morning.

"Well." Clarissa stacked the sketches, tapped them on her knee to align them and handed them back. "Those look to me like the sketches of a young woman on her way to falling in love."

Startled, May had to remind herself not to crush the papers between her fingers. Yes, Clarissa seemed to have a sixth sense, but how the heck could she see May's developing feelings for Beck in drawings of a roof garden? "What do you mean?"

"The first sketches are angular, jagged, emphasizing cement, concrete and claustrophobia. Those later ones…" She gestured gracefully toward the stack in May's grasp. "They're softer, colorful. They show a greater understanding of and appreciation for your surroundings. I had a feeling you'd fall eventually."

"But I barely know him." The words tumbled out over a panicky tightness in her chest. "Three days. It's not long enough."

Even to her ears the protest sounded overwrought. Like the last pleadings of a condemned prisoner, more frightened than sincere.

"Well." Clarissa gazed at May over the tops of her glasses. Then she took them off and folded them methodically. "I was talking about you falling in love with New York."

Crap.

May ducked her head to stare at the pictures in her lap, her face hot and undoubtedly matching the lovely red flowers in her dress.

Double crap.

"Tea?"

She peeked up to see Clarissa holding the pot questioningly. "Yes please."

"It's Darjeeling. I get the leaves from a wonderful shop in the Village on Christopher Street. They have excellent coffee, too."

May nodded. To her horror, tears were threatening to complete her humiliation.

"I'm a very good listener, you know. And for all my love of gossip, I *can* keep a secret."

A tear left the safety of May's right eye, braved the journey down her cheek to her chin and leaped into her teacup where it landed with a plop, and was absorbed by the excellent Darjeeling from Christopher Street. "I'm sorry. It's all a little confusing."

"Love is always confusing, dear. It's powerful, mysterious, and often a giant pain in the ass. Have a cookie."

May laughed, brushed away the tear remnants, and took a cookie, buttery and half-dipped in chocolate. "I'm not the woman he thinks I am. All this week I've been pretending to be worldly and sophisticated and experienced, and I'm not any of those things."

"Ah, I see." Clarissa sipped her tea and bit into a finger sandwich. "Well I *am* worldly and sophisticated and experienced, and therefore I can tell you with utter confidence that you can't possibly pretend to be something you're not."

"But I've never done anything, gone anywhere. I've never even tried to be this way before." Except when she was a terribly shy girl…

"Now you have. And if he's still coming around, you must have done very well, my dear. If you're attempting something truly outside your comfort level or contrary to your inner nature, it's not going to work for either of you."

"But I'm not—"

"Did you get the present from Trevor this morning?"

She grimaced. "Fur-trimmed? Orange?"

"Bingo." Clarissa crunched a few nuts as if she wished they were Trevor's. "Planning to model it for Beck tonight?"

"God, no."

"Exactly. Because it's not you, no matter how you look at it. Or not look at it, which is infinitely preferable. If you'll pardon me for being a horrendous buttinsky, I think you're uncovering part of yourself you never let out to taste the air until now. How many dull contented-with-next-to-nothing people do you know who'd accept a week in a place like Hush in the first place?"

"I…" May frowned. "…don't know."

"I think you do."

"But that was because my boyfriend of six years broke up with me and I went a little nuts. This was way out of character for me."

"Not at all. That's my point. The only thing that amazes me is how you could have suppressed your true nature for so long. I'm guessing this boyfriend of yours was the culprit?"

"Dan?" May laughed, not really amused and surprised how hastily she was rushing to defend him. "He was hardly the oppressive type. But he was—is—a very magnetic and dynamic person, and I…"

She was going to say, "am not" but something in Clarissa's eyes turned sharp, as if she'd throw hot tea in May's face if she put herself down any more. And come to think of it, why was she so desperate to paint herself exactly as dull as Dan had informed her she was, when she didn't even agree with him and hadn't acted that way since she met Trevor?

A faint glow started in a too-long unexplored dark

corner of her brain. Or had her transformation started sooner? Right after she and Dan broke up?

"What I want to know, dear, is why you are desperately trying to hang on to the old image of yourself rather than embracing the new when you wear it so well?"

May put her cookie down on the saucer, thinking of the night before at Exhibit A, of how hard she'd tried to be the way she saw herself in Wisconsin, and how dismally she'd failed, and how much trouble she'd taken to beat herself up for it all evening.

Oh, my goodness.

"I have a proposition for you."

May picked up her cookie again and popped it into her mouth, because not even the most profound self-exploration should stand in the way of butter and chocolate. "What's that?"

"I'm finding it harder to do my job with the same enthusiasm I used to. I'd like more time to enjoy the city, maybe do a little more traveling in the years ahead while I'm still healthy and strong. Why don't you stay in New York, I'll take you on as an assistant, and you can see what happens with Beck."

May picked up her teacup, took a sip of tea, put her teacup carefully back on its saucer and helped herself to a sandwich. Because salmon and watercress should definitely get in the way of her brain trying to wrap itself around what Clarissa had just proposed. This was all way too much to take in at once.

And yet…she didn't seem to be rushing to say no. Did she….

"Even if…I mean…well for one thing…there's no way I can afford it."

"You could stay with me at first, there's plenty of room. Hush pays quite well, you'd do fine."

The sandwich was delicious, fine-crumbed bread, salmon, dill and cream cheese, and the tart peppery contrast of watercress to cut through the richness. May tried to concentrate on the flavors, on chewing, on swallowing, and instead, drifted off into a fantasy of herself commuting amid a crowd of New Yorkers, blissfully tending the roof garden at HUSH, even more blissfully spending the occasional—or frequent—night rolling in the sheets with Beck.

Mmm.

The salmon went down the wrong pipe and she had to swig tea to avoid choking. Abrupt end of daydream.

Was that a sign? It had to be. This was all a nice dream, but she had a job back home, she still hadn't managed to kill off the vision of a life with Dan—maybe a retooled life, maybe reinvented with this new knowledge of herself to give him the excitement he wanted. Those things were real.

She put her hand to her chest and cleared her throat, grateful to the tea for rescuing her from a coughing fit. "The thing is, my mother followed thrills, and she discovered thrills weren't what they were cracked up to be. I did the same with Trevor, and look how that turned out. The week with Beck has been amazing, but Hush Hotel is not exactly reality. Life is life, wherever you live it. Same problems here that there were in Oshkosh, only more expensive."

"Ah, yes, your mother who wanted to be a Rockette and went back to Wisconsin with your father." Clarissa smiled and leaned forward, eyes very wide and very blue. "There is a lesson to be learned from that story, but if you'll forgive me, I think you learned the wrong one."

May held the last bite of sandwich suspended between her saucer and her mouth. "I don't see how."

"Try looking at it this way. Maybe your mother left to follow the thrill not when she came to New York to be a Rockette." Clarissa leaned forward and tapped May's knee with a long slender finger. "But when she left New York…to be with your father."

BECK SHOVED his chair back from the desk in his room. Chapter Seven glowed on his laptop, the cursor blinking in the same spot he'd left it two hours ago. Hell, the whole day had been like this.

He was blocked. In all his years of writing—over seven—this had never happened to him. Not even close. Mack had inhabited his brain night and day, plots and images and characters had arrived without fail. Whenever Beck sat down to work, the words and scenes had burst out like bulls from a rodeo chute. Or okay, some days like slugs out of a starting gate. But something had always made it onto the page.

Last night he'd come back from the date with May at Exhibit A and again written like a man possessed. Mack's scene with not-Susie—Beck still couldn't name her to his satisfaction—poured out onto the page, with Mack confident, in control, the sex thrilling and physically satisfying. Then out of the blue his heroine had locked her lips onto Mack's and Mack had been lost. Whatever emotional distance Beck's hero had been able to maintain vanished along with his sexual control.

The words and images had been strong, masculine and infinitely tender; they'd come to Beck effortlessly, the same way they had after May had pleasured herself in his room. No question May was a powerful muse, tuning him in to feelings his hero needed to feel.

He'd faxed the pages to Alex, and in a phone call this morning, she'd practically orgasmed herself.

Today, the opposite. Today Beck wanted to write a scene where Mack started admitting to himself and to Whatsername, that he was getting in deep. And…nothing. Not a word worth keeping. Everything sounded clichéd, contrived or like a high school freshman creative-writing assignment. A bad one. By an untalented student. With the flu.

At this rate, Mack wouldn't be falling in love and Beck would never reach the end of these revisions. His amazing beginning would fizzle out in an unconvincing scene where Mack would blurt out, "I…I…I love you," and readers the world over would groan and want to hurl.

The worst part? The words were in him to describe this thing, to do it right, the words and the emotions. He knew it. Just out of his reach, what he wanted to say sat like an eager puppy barking to be let out of his locked crate. Why the damn door was locked in the first place and how to get the key—well if he knew that, he wouldn't be blocked.

Frankly, it was scaring the crap out of him.

He dragged himself to the window and looked out at the sunshine, feeling like a convict allowed one last glimpse of freedom.

As if all that weren't enough, during the unending agony of this mental meltdown, he couldn't stop thinking about May.

Since when was any woman's pull strong enough to interfere with his work? Hell, he could work in the middle of Grand Central Station, with people on either side of him having loud cell-phone conversations. When he was really into a story, he could work at an outdoor café, with horns honking, pedestrians whooping it up, waiters bumping into his chair. He'd even been known, on one occasion he was less than proud of, to work during a date, when an idea wouldn't leave him alone.

As he recalled, his date had not been amused.

May Ellison was like the character of a yet-to-be-written guaranteed bestseller, who wouldn't leave his mind. Especially not the strobe-stuttered image of her staring at the posing couple at Exhibit A, lips parted, eyes glazed, hand expertly working his cock.

He'd called her twice today, left a message the second time asking if she'd see him tonight. For all he'd gotten done today, he should have just asked her to spend the day with him. He could have shown her New York; they could have gone out to eat, had a real date, instead of kink in the hotel, not that he'd trade a second of any of that.

She hadn't called back, and instead of shrugging it off—after all, tomorrow was her last day here, so what could they really start?—he'd fretted like a hen, like the women he'd dated had fretted over him, annoying himself like crazy in the process.

Cluck.

She'd seemed upset last night, maybe he'd said something wrong, though he couldn't imagine what. Maybe his clumsy attempts to try and articulate his feelings had scared her, or she simply didn't share them and was doing him a favor by backing off before he got in deeper. And yet—the way she looked at him, the way she'd kissed him… He wasn't out of hope.

She was still the same fascinating mystery to him, a combination of seductive and innocent, like a girl-next-door stripper. But instead of trying to decide which side was real, and which put on, he was starting to think that May was a genuine combination of both. A combination that clearly held a powerful attraction for him.

He slammed both hands to the window and looked out. May had something to do with this block. She was the key. He knew it; he just hadn't wanted to look too closely at what that signified in the context of this deeply emotional scene he wanted to write for Mack. She was screwing up his mind, but she was also making possible this new depth in his writing...and in himself. And like a kid who gets a taste of a cake and wants another and another, and then the whole piece, he craved her, to find out more about Mack, and more about himself.

Across the street, down at the end of the block, a slender blonde in a white flowered sundress caught his eye, and his heart threatened to leap out of his chest. She walked slowly, gracefully, pausing now and then to gaze in a shop window. A man turned to watch her walk past. Beck's fists clenched, then pushed hard against the glass, propelling him back into the room. Without thinking why, or what or how, he scooped up his key card and his wallet, threw open the door, and strode quickly down the hall for the elevator.

10

Note on housekeeping board:

*Anyone who cleans or turns-down 1457, check out
the sketch of the HUSH roof garden. Gorgeous!
Wish we could have it down here to look at!*

MAY STOPPED in front of a shop window teasing pas-
sersby with its elegant display of handbags and shoes
at what she was sure would be heart-stopping prices.
That much money would probably keep her in grocer-
ies for a month back in Oshkosh. She lingered, staring
at a pair of bright red pumps, not so much fascinated by
the merchandise as delaying returning to the hotel. Her
visit with Clarissa had unleashed some of the adventuress in her, and she wanted to see more of New York. Do
more. The hotel had meant safety all week, but today…
today it came closer to representing confinement.
Granted, the most luxurious and pampering confinement she'd ever experienced, but she craved something
different right now.

Like…what? Could she go out in New York tonight
on her own? Or suggest to Beck they leave the hotel and
go out on the town?

It sounded good. No, actually, it sounded wonderful. But seeing Beck meant confronting her feelings, confronting who she was, making choices, making decisions....

She lifted her arms in surrender and let them flop back down so the bag containing her sketch pad bonked against her side. All of which was enough to make her think about running home to Dan and begging him to take her back.

And what kind of adventuress did *that* make her?

A fake one. Who handled stress or risk by wanting to run to safety, whether that meant staying away from Beck, or longing for the carefully controlled peace of her Wisconsin existence. She might get to the point where New York didn't overwhelm her anymore, but for all Clarissa's assertions to the contrary, May didn't belong here. She needed calm.

She turned from the window and nearly bumped into Beck.

"May." He said her name in a serious, intense way as if discovering her on this street was the best thing that had ever happened to him, and that ever could happen to him. And if her pounding heart and the grin she couldn't control were anything to go by, May was quite sure it felt like the best thing that had ever happened to her, too.

So what did that tell her about needing calm? She didn't know. And was tired of trying to figure it all out.

"Shopping?" He gestured at a painfully pointy-toed pair of shoes in the window she'd been ogling.

"Not me. I was having tea with Clarissa."

"Heading back to the hotel now?"

May managed a guilty smile. "I was sort of avoiding it."

"And sort of avoiding me?"

She sort of had been, but faced with him, so large and confident, eyes warm, breeze rippling his hair like a wheatfield, her reasons seemed forced and artificial. "Not avoiding you. Just wanting to be out and about for a change."

He grinned and reached to touch her hair, followed the line of her cheek down to her chin, leaving a warm, touched trail on her skin that made her want to jump him right here in the street. "Would you like to go out and about with me, Ms. Ellison?"

She laughed. God, yes. Of course she did. How had she managed once again to make a simple situation so complicated? This was her last night in New York, and her only chance to see anything of the city on this trip since she'd been such a weenie so far about venturing out.

More than that, she wasn't going to worry about who she was or how she was acting, or how she felt or how he felt or what would happen tomorrow, or—

Okay, May.

She'd be whatever came out and see how it felt. "I'd love to."

"Let's go."

"Now?" But she was dressed for an afternoon tea, and her—

"You have some other pressing engagement?"

She laughed. Why did she let everything send her into a panic? "Not a one. I'm just not done up for an evening out."

"You look beautiful."

Beautiful? Wearing only half the new fabulous makeup she'd tried out this week, lipstick worn off and hair blown wild? "Well, thank you."

"I saw you from my window." He leaned forward to murmur in her ear. "Every man in New York was turning to check you out."

She pulled back, beaming, even though she knew he was exaggerating. "No way."

"Why do you think I'm out here?" He held his hands out, palms up. "I was afraid one of them would make you a better offer."

"There *is* no better offer."

He chuckled and the mischievous childlike dimple jumped in to crease his grown-up face. "Okay then."

"Okay then."

He turned her around and took her hand; his felt large and strong, and May experienced the extreme giddiness that only being with someone you're madly infatuated with can bring on.

Beck pulled a cell phone out of his pocket and held it up. "Want to play hunt the cancellation?"

She grinned, wanting to laugh out loud from the sheer joy of being at his side. Whatever he wanted to do was fine by her. The way she felt right now, the evening couldn't possibly be anything but wonderful. "What's that?"

"See if anyone has cancelled his reservation at a fabulous restaurant so we can grab it."

"Oooh, that sounds like a fun game. I'd love to play."

"Excellent."

She walked alongside, bumping him sort of accidentally once in a while and listening while he dialed and spoke to various employees of the city's finest. Le Bernardin, Nougatine, Craft, and finally…

"Bingo. Cancellation at Nobu, we're on."

"Nobu?"

"You like fish? Sushi?"

"I only had it once, but yes, I did like it."

He gave her a curious look and she realized she'd blown some of her Veronica cover, but what the heck. She was going home tomorrow and had nothing left to lose. "This is a fabulous place. And I know the perfect spot for a drink beforehand, not too far from the restaurant."

She smiled up at him. "Obviously I have the perfect date."

"Obviously." They ambled over to Fifth Avenue chatting easily. On Fifth, Beck took it upon himself to instruct her in the fine art of hailing a cab.

Step in street. Raise arm. Look nonchalant, not hopeful.

Feeling only a little self-conscious and awkward, May reeled in a lovely plump yellow one on her second try, which made her swell with inane pride.

The cab took them south, past Lord and Taylor's, May's mother's favorite shopping spot—she'd often described their fabulous window exhibits at Christmastime—then farther south where traffic slowed and Beck pointed out the Empire State Building. The Empire State Building! She'd traveled along this same route only a few hours ago on her way to tea and had missed it. Why hadn't she come down here to see it? Why hadn't she walked over to check out the theater district on Broadway? Why hadn't she gone up to see Radio City Music Hall where her mother had worked? What was the matter with her? She was in *New York!*

And like earlier today, the crowds didn't seem hostile, the air didn't seem thick, the streets didn't seem dirty. Instead of suffocation, the buildings promised fascinating interiors and glimpses into people's lives.

Was she getting used to New York? Falling in love

with it as Clarissa said? Or had her earlier suspicion proved true, that the world could be nothing but wonderful when Beck was with her?

The cab continued down Fifth Avenue, past gorgeous old buildings whose ground floors housed nationally recognized chain stores, delis, shoe boutiques—did New Yorkers do anything but shop? Then the arch of the monument in Washington Square Park came into view. The cab turned left, then right onto Broadway into what Beck told her was Soho, with antique shops and churches, more upscale stores, and tall high-heeled model-gorgeous women strutting around holding shopping bags. Another right, another left, and they were at their destination: the green-awninged entrance to a place called...

"The Bubble Lounge?"

Beck grinned and paid the cabdriver. "A very chic Laundromat. I thought we could watch spinning underwear and get in the mood."

May burst into laughter as she got out of the cab. "Oh, baby. You know how to show a woman a good time."

He followed her onto the sidewalk, took her hand and twisted it gently behind her so she came up flush against him. He bent close and she caught her breath and a whiff of his aftershave. "I want to show you the best time you've ever had, May. And then I want to get you alone and show you an even better one. No floor show, no audience, no toys. Okay?"

Okay. She mouthed the word, intending to speak, but no sound came out. Her eyes were trapped by his, her body light, sparking energy. Then he kissed her right there on the sidewalk with half of New York going by. Not a gentle kiss, either, a long, hot knee-melting kiss that made her want to wrap her arms around his neck and kiss him back without caring who saw. So she damn well did.

"Hey, man, get a room."

The shout and ensuing teenage laughter broke them apart, luckily before May embarrassed herself by humping his leg or something equally crazy. He took her so far out of herself she didn't even recognize who she was. And the more he did it and the further she went, the more she liked the new bolder, more sensual person she was with Beck. If only it would last.

He released her and they walked—okay, he walked, she floated—through the glass door and into—oh, my goodness—the Bubble Lounge. Not a Laundromat. High ceilings, dim lighting, terra-cotta floor tiles, rich red-and-gold decor, posters and prints and old illustrations of fine bottles, floor-to-ceiling mahogany shelves, velvet sofas, oriental rugs, voluptuous draperies... Despite its kitschy name, The Bubble Lounge appeared to be an homage to romantic elegance. And champagne. *Mmm.*

The hour was too early for the after-work crowd, so they were able to pick a plush red sofa adjacent to a large window. From three hundred varieties of champagne, Beck ordered one, which came in two flutes, delicate and cold, streams of tiny bubbles continuously scurrying up for air.

"Here's to New York." She lifted her glass and clinked with Beck.

"To New York. And to meeting you."

What you think is me. She faked a smile and took her first sip, smiled more genuinely in pleasure at its nutty clean taste, and suddenly couldn't stand that she'd tried to lead him on all week to think she was something other than herself. "It's nice to get out of the hotel."

"It is."

"I spent too much time there this week. The truth was…" She started to put her champagne down on the low round table in front of their couch, then decided she might need it for fortification. "I was chicken. Not brave enough to go out on my own."

He frowned, and she braced herself for *What's so terrifying about a city?* "You should have asked me, I would have been happy to show you around."

Was he just being polite? "You were working."

"I could have given you directions, survival tips, put you in a cab to a museum or store or show or landmark, and picked you up after. Or taken my laptop and waited while you had fun. I can work anywhere." He looked pained, as if her lost week here was somehow his responsibility and he'd failed her.

Which wasn't at all the response May was expecting. "No, no, it was my fault for being so timid."

"New York's not for sissies." He drank more champagne, apparently unconcerned by her supposed-to-be-damning confession.

Irritation pricked her. Didn't he get it? "It's a far cry from Wisconsin."

"Tell me about Wisconsin."

"It's quieter, slower, less…well less everything. The town I live in is small. Not exactly up on the latest trends. You'd probably find it dull."

"Do you?"

"We'll see when I go back." She shrugged. "Up until this week, no. But I'm a different person there."

"Really." He quirked one eyebrow, then leaned in

close. "Why don't you stay in New York longer, another week or two, or a month. Get to know the city, see how you like it. Do all the sightseeing you missed this week. See what kind of person you are then."

Her breath misfired and she had to try again. "I'd...lose my job."

"Then quit and move here."

May attempted a laugh, sure he wasn't serious, half-wishing he was. "Pick up my entire life and relocate after four days?"

"Sure." He grinned, then his expression turned serious. "You can stay with me until you find a place of your own."

"A kept woman."

"I'd keep you very well, May."

She hid her confusion in a long sip of champagne. This *was* a joke, wasn't it? "Actually, that's the second offer I've had today. Clarissa said I should move here, too. She even offered me her job."

"There you go. It's settled."

May smiled at him, and he smiled back, and the smile went on too long and started to spark something very hot between them—and then something sweet and even more thrilling than heat. Between a celebrity author and a simple girl from Oshkosh—was she imagining it? Willing it into existence?

She dropped her eyes and drank more champagne, probably downing it too fast to appreciate, but at this point it seemed a necessity rather than a mere beverage. The same excitement she'd felt with Clarissa at the thought of living in New York hit her, only since Beck mentioned it, the feeling came closer to exhilaration.

Steady, May. He meant the invitation as a compliment, the way you'd tell a houseguest you'd particularly enjoyed that you wished she wasn't leaving, even though you knew perfectly well if she stayed much longer, you'd both go nuts. This compliment she'd treasure forever, along with the rose petal she'd saved and remembered to transfer to her suitcase this morning, along with all the memories from the week.

"There is one thing I really want to know about you, May." Beck put his champagne down on the table.

Uh-oh. She tried not to look as if she was bracing herself for execution. "Just one?"

"What's the story with this guy you were supposed to meet at Hush?"

May took a deep breath, loosening her grip on her glass to avoid snapping the slender stem. If she told him honestly, there'd be no Veronica illusion left. But she'd come too far in how she felt about him to do otherwise. "That was pretty stupid of me."

"How so?"

"He came to Wisconsin, where I work as assistant to the dean of the business school. We hit it off, and he invited me here. The one and only boyfriend of my life had just ended our six-year relationship, and I was angry and hurting, and a little out of my mind, the way you are when someone dumps you."

"I can imagine." He said the words looking blank. She should have expected that. He undoubtedly did all the dumping.

"So I agreed to spend the week with him. Then he didn't show, and then I found out from Clarissa that he was married, which I could have pieced together myself if I had half a brain. So after all that, I was glad he didn't show and felt naive and ridiculous for having gotten myself into it in the first place. The end."

There. She dared a glance up at Beck and found him staring at her with a look of satisfaction, as if he'd just solved a puzzle that had been tormenting him. Which he undoubtedly had concerning her fake Veronica act. Women like Veronica wouldn't have needed Clarissa to spell out in block letters that Trevor was married. Nor would they rush to justify a scheduled sexathon as a reaction to their boyfriend dumping them.

"Sounds like you needed to get away."

"I guess. But it was pretty cowardly."

He cocked his head questioningly. "Why?"

Wasn't it obvious? "I was running away from the pain instead of dealing with it."

"Seems to me you were taking steps to start over."

"With a married man?"

"You didn't know he was married."

"I should have."

"Why are you being so hard on yourself?" He took her champagne from her and put it on the table, next to his, then took both of her hands and held them. "You were hurt, badly. Instead of staying home, collapsed and sniffling, you took a risk, jumped at what you hoped was a chance for new happiness, even temporary. I'd say that's pretty brave."

"I'd say it was irresponsible."

"Only because of how it ended up. What if you'd come to New York to meet me?"

She smiled, a champagne-assisted warm glow lighting her up at the mere thought. "That would have been much smarter."

"See?"

"But still out of character."

"Hmm." He studied her as if he was testing a mind-reading device. "Then what is your character?"

"I'm not impulsive. Not a risk-taker. Not particularly daring sexually."

His eyebrows shot up. "Um…"

She blushed as if it were her last chance ever to blush again and she wanted to do it up right. "I mean usually. This week was definitely not usual. In Oshkosh, I'm pretty…normal and predictable and—"

"Then why do I think you're the most exciting woman I've ever met?"

May's jaw opened and shut. The most what? "Because…this week I haven't been myself."

"Who have you been?"

When she didn't answer, his fingers tightened on her hands; he leaned forward, his gaze so focused on her he looked almost angry. "The things I've seen you do this week are not things an average predictable woman would do. And if you go back to Wisconsin and to this boyfriend who has made you feel average and predictable, you'll be committing a major crime."

His wink took some of the intensity out of his words and May chuckled, more nervous than amused. What made him and Clarissa assume Dan had kept some kind of lid on her real self? She'd never felt that way with him. Just protected and safe and…loved. "That sounds pretty dire."

"It would be dire. A damn waste of a fabulous woman." He let go of her hands and before she could feel the loss of physical contact, he tangled his ankles with hers and leaned in so close she could see the tiny feathery patterns of his iris. "I know I won't be able to convince you to stay now, May. So I'll leave it until you have more champagne in you and I get you alone. Then I'll make you so hot and so breathless I'll be able to extract all kinds of promises you wouldn't make to me now in a million years."

She wanted to laugh again, to keep the moment light, but the idea of him driving her so crazy she'd promise to stay was making her hot and breathless already. "I can't move here."

"Why? Forget the practical stuff. Concentrate on the big picture."

She studied the crinkled edges of her napkin, unable to figure out how to respond to that. Right now he thought she was the most exciting woman he'd ever met. She did feel exciting around him, and the circumstances and the wonderful freeing atmosphere at HUSH had made it easier for her to cut loose. But how long before that thrill wore off? How long would he hang around once he realized she was just a normal nice person, with a love of routine and home and family? A woman who felt that most of the time sex should be part of a love relationship, and that a love relationship should lead to marriage and family.

"I don't know if I can handle New York."

"Why not?"

She paused, considering her answer even though her statement had been designed only to throw him off the real trail. But the crowds hadn't seemed too bad today, maybe even energizing. And the lack of green—she'd found bits of it where she could escape and she hadn't even explored Central Park yet. Rude behavior had alternated with friendly and helpful. Weird people today seemed less like threats and more like the spice of life variety gives. And it wasn't as if Oshkosh was exclusively stocked with saints.

"I don't think...I..."

"Tell me about a typical day for you in Wisconsin—where in Wisconsin, by the way?"

"Oshkosh."

"Tell me about a typical day in Oshkosh."

She nodded. Good idea. Now he'd see what she was talking about. "I wake up and go to work—"

"Breakfast?"

"You want to know what I have for breakfast?"

"Yes."

"O-kay. I have cereal."

"Sweet cereal? Marshmallow-y cereal?"

She made a face. "No way. Shredded wheat or cornflakes or Cheerios. With milk—"

"Skim? Two percent?"

She laughed. "Skim. And wheat germ. Bananas in the winter and strawberries or blueberries in the summer. I shower. I make my lunch—" She held up a hand to stave off his question.

"Sandwich or salad, fruit and a cookie. I drive to work. I work. I swim at the college pool either on my lunch hour or after work. I come home, I eat dinner, read, sometimes rent a movie and go to bed. The next day I do it again. On weekends I clean or read or go out with friends."

There. She waited for him to start spewing champagne in disgust.

"Okay." He drained his glass and set it down, rubbed his hands together, as if he was accepting a challenge. "Here's my day as a wild and worldly sophisticated New Yorker. I get up. I shower. I eat whole-grain toast with peanut butter and jam, sometimes pancakes or eggs. On Sundays I have a croissant from a bakery a few blocks over. I write in the mornings. I take a walk. I buy a sandwich at the corner deli, chips and a pickle and a candy bar or brownie or oatmeal raisin cookie. I come home, write in the afternoon, work out at the gym, cook my dinner, read, watch TV and go to bed. Occasionally I eat with my family or go see a movie with a friend. Sound familiar?"

She nodded, playing with her glass, tipping it one way and the other, watching the bubbles chase each other to get to the surface.

His hand covered her free one. "We live in different cities, but we don't live different lives. I have no doubt you could handle New York."

She looked up and met his eyes and something much more than lust passed between them. His confidence in her made her feel powerful and capable and…well, as if she was Veronica for real. Even as she was admitting she was May.

"I squeeze the toothpaste from the bottom."

He winced. "Middle."

"Toilet paper over the top."

"Agreed."

She exhaled exaggerated relief. "Hate soap scum in the shower, but leave shoes lying around."

"Obsessively scrub countertops but let the kitchen floor get gray before I'll mop it."

"Don't vacuum under the couch more than a few times a year."

"Keep leftovers in little containers until they get moldy, then I throw them away."

She started to giggle. "Rarely wash windows."

"Obsessive about uncluttered work space."

"Obsessive about neat dresser drawers."

"Pay bills on time."

"Pay bills on time."

"Never talk to women about how I feel about them."

May frowned. "I generally—"

"May, don't leave New York until we've figured out what's going on between us. This is different from anything I've felt before and I want to know why."

She blinked. "You just said you never talk to women about—"

"I know." He tugged gently on a lock of her hair. "That's why I don't want you to go."

Her mouth fell open a little before she noticed and closed it. He was serious about wanting her to move? Even now, when she'd taken off the Veronica veil and revealed what lay beneath? Did this mean…what *did* this mean? "I…don't know what to say."

"Just think about it, that's all I ask."

She nodded. The waiter showed up; Beck squeezed May's hand, glanced at his watch, then paid over her protests, and led them back out into the street.

They walked the few blocks to Nobu, down West Broadway. Everywhere May looked there were specialty food shops, bakeries, ethnic restaurants, delis, how did everyone in the city stay so thin? How did anyone keep from spending all his money just walking around during lunch hour? She wanted to go into every single store and restaurant, try everything, compare, pick favorites. Then move on to another neighborhood and do it again. Maybe Beck was right. Maybe she *could* handle New York.

They arrived at Nobu and went inside, changing places with a laughing couple just leaving. The interior of the restaurant resembled a geometric forest; regularly spaced "trees" with twin trunks spread upward into constructed branches that evoked inverted umbrellas. The floor, walls and ceilings were rosy blond wood, the chairs made a pretty, dark contrast. Heavenly smells permeated and every dish May peeked at on the wooden tables they passed looked both beautiful and delicious.

They settled into their table and ordered more champagne—who could ever get enough? She'd have to stock her apartment in Oshkosh with a few cases to get her through the winter.

The image appealed—briefly. Every time she drank it now she'd think of this week here with Beck. Maybe it wouldn't taste quite the same. Undoubtedly it wouldn't.

Beck toasted her again, his blue-gray eyes starting to be so dear to her she wasn't sure how she could say goodbye to them, let alone the rest of him. "I could make this a habit, how about you?"

"Same." She clinked her glass to his, trying to banish the touch of sadness creeping into her mood.

He leaned across the table and kissed her, kissed her again, drew his tongue gently across her lower lip and sat back, looking at her as if she were the Mona Lisa or the Pietà, or the eighth wonder of the ancient world. Her sadness immediately succumbed to the wave of happiness and warmth flooding her. There just couldn't be anything that felt better than this. Except maybe his naked body flush against hers in cotton sheets.

Was she nuts to give up a chance at love with this man?

"Middle name?"

She blinked, then realized what he meant a second later. "Hope. Yours?"

"Hope."

"Your middle name is Hope, too?"

He laughed. "I was enjoying yours. May Hope Ellison. I like that."

"Thanks." Not as much as she liked hearing it on his lips. She raised her brows expectantly. "Yours?"

"Charles."

"Oh, a great name. My brother's in fact."

"Really. Favorite movie kiss?"

"That's easy. Spencer Tracy and Katharine Hepburn in *Woman of the Year*."

"The scene where she's invited him to the airport?"

May sighed dramatically and quoted. "'I was sort of hoping that you'd kiss me goodbye.'"

"And he shoots his arm out and grabs her to him."

"Yes." May patted her heart. "Wonderful. What's yours?"

"In *Witness,* when Harrison Ford and Kelly McGinnis rush at each other. I was thirteen and thought she was totally hot."

May laughed, retroactively jealous of Kelly McGinnis. "Favorite food?"

"Peanut butter. I could eat it every day. In fact I probably come close. Yours?"

"Chocolate chip cookies."

"With nuts, I hope?"

"Of course."

"Eat them every day?"

She mimed a large stomach and shook her head. "Wish I could, though."

"Favorite sport."

"Packers football. You?"

"Yankees baseball."

"Favorite thing to do when it rains."

"Hmm. That depends." He lifted an eyebrow and gave her a lazy sex look. "Are you there?"

"Let's say yes."

He leaned forward, making the air between them buzz with intimacy. "Then I'd want to take your clothes off, slowly…one item at a time. Taste every inch of your skin and make love to you until you can no longer stand, make you come so many times you can't anymore."

May swallowed the champagne she'd held in her mouth while listening, sure she'd be able to do no more than whisper a response. "That would be fine."

"I don't know if I can wait through dinner before I'm inside you, May."

Oh, my word. She'd never ever, ever felt anything like this daring dangerous thrill. A thrill that went clear through to her heart. Did it touch his, as well? "Really?"

"It's going to be tough. My chances of survival are—"

"Hello and welcome to Nobu." The waitress bowed slightly. "Do you have any questions about the menu?"

Beck snapped into polite charm over May's barely suppressed giggle and ordered the tasting menu for both of them.

The dinner was sublime. Course after perfect tiny course arrived, ingredients and combinations May had sometimes never even heard of let alone imagined. It was by far the best meal she'd ever had—and not just because of the food.

Now that she didn't have to pretend to be anything but who she was, she and Beck talked easily about everything. He told her about growing up in New York, about his family and their restaurant, about his struggles getting published, and his struggle writing earlier that day.

She told him about her isolated childhood, her day-dreams, how she watched old movies incessantly, how she met Dan and he became her world for so many years, about her mom's adventure here in New York and her dad's ensuing rescue. She couldn't help a growing sense of awe that her life and childhood interested him so much, that stories Dan knew by heart found such entrancing new life.

Maybe it was simply a new ear, but she felt as if Beck really heard, not just listened, really took the details into account in the picture of her he must be forming. And even as that picture formed, he showed no signs of pulling away, didn't look at his watch, didn't ogle the many more beautiful women around the restaurant, as Dan always did.

Why had she held herself back for so long? Why had she had so little confidence that her true self would appeal to him? Seeing her real self, getting to know her better, would that deepen his feelings to where he could see a future for them out of bed as well as in it?

"Now." She pushed her cup of tea to the side and leaned her forearms on the otherwise empty table. "Tell me more about you. I've talked way too much."

"But it's interesting."

"And you must be ten times more. Tell me about writing. The process."

His eyes lit up like those of a kid about to open his favorite present. "Writing fiction is the best job in the world."

"No downside?"

"As in any job, there's drudgery and frustration, like today, but those moments where you nail a scene, or the best part, when you turn in a completed manuscript you're pleased with, those are incredibly satisfying highs. It's so much a part of me, what emerges. And if it's good, and people react favorably, then it's a compliment about who I am as well as what I've done."

May nodded enthusiastically, thrilling to the emotional connection. "Yes. Yes. That's how I feel about drawing."

"You draw?"

"Oh. Well…yes. It's not a big deal." She cringed. Why had she mentioned it? She wasn't remotely on his level creatively speaking. "Did I tell you I went to visit Clarissa today?"

He gave her that amused half grin which acknowledged her change of subject without objecting. "Yes, you mentioned it. She's a fascinating person. I get the sense she was quite a femme fatale in her time."

"We had this fabulous tea."

"Where she told you to move here, and take her job."

"She wants to retire or go part-time for a while, and her assistant left to get married."

"It's fate, May. Clarissa's job. Me." He winked. "It's what you're meant to do."

She rolled her eyes over a smile, but her stomach—besides being full of excellent food—was full of shivery excitement. The idea that this fantasy could go on longer… Was she really ready to go home tomorrow?

But what would she be staying for? Wasn't it better to leave while the infatuation was still shiny and perfect? Before any tarnish set in? What would she have to give up to move here and what would she be stuck with if Beck grew tired of her?

"Say you'll stay."

"Beck, I can't."

"Then say you'd like to. At least in theory."

She smiled. That she could do. "I'd certainly like to in theory."

"I'll take that for now."

The waitress brought the check and hovered, glancing nervously at Beck while he signed. "Excuse me. I saw your name. Could you...could I get your autograph for my boyfriend? To John?"

Beck nodded graciously and held his pen up, at the ready. "What would you like me to sign?"

"Oh." She looked around blankly.

"I have paper." May reached into the bag for her sketch pad and pulled out a clean sheet. "Here."

She passed it to Beck; he signed with a flourish and handed the autograph to the nearly swooning waitress with a smile that faded after she left.

"Okay, May. I let it go before, but no longer. Are those your sketches?"

She nodded reluctantly. "Clarissa asked me to bring them along today."

"I see." He beckoned with his hand, like a stern parent wanting a forbidden toy given up. "Hand them over."

She wrinkled her nose and complied. Then had to endure the torture of him looking at her work, while she sat there and folded her napkin and sipped water and waited for judgment. *Ugh.*

"May, these are really good." He handed back the sketch pad and gave her a look of admiration tempered by exasperation. "What the hell made you think you were dull and predictable?"

She stared down at a tiny puddle of broth left at her place. Dan had been the first to verbalize it...but she'd always felt that way, hadn't she?

She tried to look up at Beck, but only made it as far as his chin. "You don't make me feel either dull or predictable."

He reached across the table and lifted her chin so she had to meet his eyes. "And what does that tell you?"

She knew what she wanted it to be telling her, and what she wanted him to feel, too. *That we're destined to be together forever.* That after enjoying this thrilling start, instead of moving on to another relationship, he'd see love, marriage, babies and forever in their future. "I don't know. Tell me something more about you."

"Okay." He ran his thumb over her lips, making her want to sneak her tongue out and taste his skin—so she did, and it was smooth and slightly salty from soy sauce. "What else do you want to know?"

"Everything."

He started to smile, then abruptly, his grin froze, his thumb stopped moving across her lips, his eyes went distant.

May held her breath. What? What?

"I have an idea." He took his hand back across the table. "If you're sure you want to know more about me…"

"Yes. Yes, I do."

He laughed, shaking his head. "I can't believe I'm even considering this."

"What?" She laughed, partly from nerves, partly because whatever it was, she knew she'd enjoy it if they were together.

"May Hope Ellison." He clasped his hands on the table and leaned forward. "How would you like to go to my little brother's birthday party?"

11

MAY EXITED the cab behind Beck onto West 55th Street, not at all sure what to expect. This wasn't exactly like taking her home to meet his parents, was it? And yet…in fact, he was taking her to meet his parents. And his brothers. And their significant others. And apparently aunts and uncles and cousins and friends and…so on.

All of them probably as literarily inclined and sophisticated as Beck. How the heck would she fit in? How to make a good impression? Administrative Assistant, oh yeah, now that was earthshakingly fascinating. Just the kind of woman we hoped you'd find, Beck. Forget the graduate degrees, the brilliant background in publishing or research or medicine, we just want you to bring home a secretary from Oshkosh. Seriously.

She itched to call Ginny. Beck had barely spoken all the way here. She could tell he was nervous, maybe regretting what he admitted was an impulsive offer? And *his* being nervous only made *her* more nervous. Would he end up ashamed of her?

Guess what, she'd soon find out, because here they were, walking into Cucina d'Amore restaurant—past the Closed, Private Party sign.

At least it was a casual-looking place, not white tablecloths nor terrifyingly trendy. And the soundtrack featured Dean Martin crooning "That's Amore," how intimidating could that be? The guests gathered around the bar in the back—sigh of relief, none of them looked to be turned out in the latest fashion. Or even expensive classic fashion. And there wasn't the army of people she expected, maybe a dozen, give or take. She and Beck must be late enough that the party had lost an uncle or ten.

One of the dark heads turned toward them. "Hey, it's Beck."

The roar following this announcement was so loud and so unexpected, May nearly stumbled. Beck's hand tightened around hers and she put on what she hoped was an extremely pleasant smile. That did not sound like the greeting of a crowd of elite sophisticates.

A dizzying series of introductions followed, featuring many curious but friendly stares directed at May, and a lot of jokes about the prodigal son directed at Beck. And when had he grown so tall? And what grade was he in now?

Apparently Beck didn't spend a lot of time with his family. Or at least not enough in their view. So why would he bring her?

In the chaos of new faces, she managed to fasten on his mother, who hugged her son for easily three minutes, a short, slightly plump woman with a faint Italian accent, warm eyes, pale skin and jet-black hair. Her husband, almost comically taller and with lighter coloring, seemed a man of few words, but those few were unaccented and full of affection for Beck. He must bring the decidedly un-Italian name Desmond into the mix, and undoubtedly his side of the family was responsible for Beck's non-Mediterranean appearance. Brothers Jeffrey and Zachary were both shorter than Beck, darker and handsome in a beefy obvious kind of way.

Nobody was what she expected.

"So, Beck." His brother Zachary, wearing green shorts and a loud Hawaiian shirt with parrots all over it, clapped him on the back. "What happened to get you here, your hotel burned down?"

"No." He grinned, apparently accustomed to the ribbing. "You're looking particularly swank this evening, Zach."

"Ain't I though?"

"So, what's this about?" A woman May thought was Zachary's wife pushed in under her husband's arm. "You finished your book?"

"Not yet."

"Then what are you doing here?"

He made a helpless gesture. "I'm temporarily blocked."

"You need more fiber?" This from a voice toward the back of the bar.

Beck rolled his eyes good-naturedly and laughed with everyone else, his previous tension apparently easing.

"Okay. Shut up everyone." Jeffrey, the brother whose birthday/engagement party it was, stood rather unsteadily and raised his glass. "I wan' propose a toast to the bes' big brother I ever had. And to congratulate him for bringin' a woman here tonight, who is almost as hot as my future wife."

This time the roar was of disapproval. "Sit down you bum!"

"Hey! No son of mine is going to talk to a lady like that." Mrs. Desmond grabbed Jeffrey's ear and started hauling him out of the room. A tiny woman May recognized was Mary, Jeffrey's fiancée, leaped off her stool into their path.

"Stop that!" She grabbed Mrs. Desmond's hand off her true love.

Silence descended. Apparently defying the matriarch was simply not done.

"That's *my* job now." Mary grinned widely, grabbed Jeffrey's ear herself and led him out of the room to the raucous cheers and taunts of the partygoers.

May laughed along, and caught Beck grinning down at her. "Is this what you expected?"

"Um, no." She chuckled again. "Your family is a riot."

"That's one way of putting it." He slid his arm around her and bent to murmur into her hair. "Still think New York is out of your league?"

Her laughter faded into a lovely warm stillness. Was that why he'd brought her here? To share the warmth of his family? To show her another reason she could thrive in New York?

"You brought me here to prove I'd fit in," she whispered.

"Yes, partly." He kissed her temple, his lips warm and mmm, perfect. "And because I've been an AWOL son and brother too often."

"Thank you." She struggled to keep her emotions under control. "It's one of the nicest things anyone's done for me."

"I'd like to do more, if you'll let me."

Oh, stay cool her melting heart. No one had ever taken such pains to make her feel good about herself. Or seemed to feel it was important to put her needs first. Would he go to all this trouble if he was just after a week or two or three of sex?

It didn't seem likely.

"Yo, *Beck*." A cousin of some sort, she couldn't remember. Mark? Joe? She'd lost track. "I've got a *great* idea for a story for you."

May smiled at the glazed-over look on Beck's face. Cousin Mark or Joe was followed by a few others, and then a few more, all friendly, all politely interested in May and clearly anxious to catch up with Beck.

Finally it seemed the group was thinning; even those with sure-sell plots had left Beck alone, and he twined his fingers with hers. "Ready to go?"

She nodded, hoping there was more to the evening ahead, more that involved the two of them and one room. With a bed in it. "I just need to go to the ladies'."

He pointed to a doorway around back of the bar and she made her way into the pleasant and clean two-stall facility. While she was washing her hands with heavenly lavender-scented liquid soap, another woman came in, tall, dark and stunning, with vibrant red lipstick and nails.

"You're May, right?"

May nodded, totally blanking on the woman's name, but pretty sure she belonged in the "friend of the family" category.

"I'm Angie."

"Angie, that's right, I'm sorry."

"Don't worry about it, you met everyone tonight." She took a comb out of her purse and started fussing with her medium-length hairdo. "So you're Beck's latest, huh."

May didn't know how to answer that, but she also didn't enjoy the but-not-last implication. "I guess I am."

"I was about three girlfriends ago."

May turned off the faucet and shook her hands in the

sink, wanting to fling the water on Ms. Rain-On-Your-Parade and watch her sink to the floor, screaming, "I'm melting…" She had a bad, bad feeling about where this conversation was going. Since Angie wasn't making any move to use the empty stall, she must have come in just to talk to May. Or corner her. Or pound her into emotional pulp.

Ugh. She'd only recently gotten a securely warm fuzzy feeling with Beck and she didn't want any bitter brunette cooling or defuzzing it.

"Really?" She tossed the towel into the trash and wondered how rude it would be to walk out.

"How long have you been dating?"

May hid a wince. "Four days."

Angie turned from staring at May in the mirror and stared at May in person out of two heavily made-up narrowed eyes. "Four days, huh. Well, enjoy it, you're still in the fun part. He's taking you places, showing you off. It's great, isn't it?"

Oh, for God's sake. "Then what, he turns into a pumpkin at midnight?"

"Something like that." She returned to looking in the mirror, and began fiddling with her hair, which she was taking a lot of trouble to make look exactly as she had when she walked in. "I became friends with the family so I've seen him with his girlfriends over the years. He's as predictable as the moon."

"You know, I don't really think I want to hear this."

Angie shot out a hand and grabbed May's arm. "I know, you think I'm a bitch. But I wouldn't feel right if I didn't warn you."

"Okay." May removed her arm from the red-nailed grasp, still feeling trapped. "I'm listening."

"He's a great guy don't get me wrong, but a keeper, he's not. Fun at first, then after the thrill wears off, you start feeling like you're last week's garbage." She shook her head and hardly a strand of the oversprayed hair moved. "You start noticing that he doesn't share much of himself emotionally. You start noticing that he does what he wants and you have to fit in. You start noticing that he's not always listening when you talk. And you start noticing that you're always at your place. Six months before I even knew where he lived."

"I have to go." May sped to the door, but not fast enough. Angie was apparently not finished, and her voice rose as May got farther away.

"Three years we dated, and he never said I love you, not once. You want marriage? Babies? Look somewhere else. Trust me on this."

The door shut on those choice words and May was faced with having to stroll back to Beck pretending that her entire world hadn't just threatened to crash around her. Okay, maybe the woman was bitter. And maybe her words had touched on every insecurity May had.

And maybe…she was right.

"Ready to go?" Beck smiled warmly, looking at her as if she were his lifesaving buoy in a sea of strangeness.

"Yes." She'd never been readier for anything in her life.

They said goodbyes all around, promised visits again soon, then stepped out into the blissfully fresh air and Beck hailed a cab, glancing back at May.

"You tired?"

"A little." She wasn't. Not tired, not energized, either, not happy, not sad. Sort of in suspended animation. But he'd noticed. Hadn't he? Angie said…

She couldn't keep thinking about what Angie said or she'd go nuts.

A cab stopped and she got in, staring out the window, not paying attention to the sights around her or to whatever Beck leaned forward and said to the driver.

His arm came around her; she turned and registered on his face such a look of concern, she told the ghost of Angie to take a big long hike off the edge of the Grand Canyon.

"I hope that wasn't too overwhelming."

"It was fun."

"Sometimes I feel like I must have been kidnapped by aliens and dropped into this family when they couldn't find my own again to return me." He grinned ruefully and May's heart skipped a painful beat. She had a totally irrational desire to go back into his childhood and fix everything for him. At the same time it occurred to her in spite of herself, that he didn't sound like Angie's version of a man who never shared his emotional self.

"But they're wonderful people. And obviously proud of you."

"Yes." He looked amazed, as if before tonight that hadn't been part of what he'd sensed, and her heart got even more painful for what he must have suffered. "I enjoyed myself tonight. And it meant a lot to me to have you there, May."

She opened her mouth to say "me, too," when silly female tears announced they were on the way, and she ducked her head to blink rapidly. He lifted her chin; drew her to him, stared into her eyes for a long, beautiful, terrifying moment that turned her heart half upside down, and then he kissed her. And kissed her. And kissed her. Long, slow, languid kisses that made her feel like the world was dissolving around her. His lips were imaginative, varying the pressure, sometimes involving his tongue, sometimes not, tasting every part of her mouth until not only was she a quivering mass of reawakened hormones, but her heart had turned the rest of the way upside down, and she experienced again that sweet, nearly unbearable ache that made her want to all-out bawl even though she felt no conscious reason to be sad.

"I can't wait to get you alone."

"Same here." She curled into his side, thinking it might be possible to die of happiness. Regardless of what happened the next day, tonight was going to be about her and about Beck, exactly as she'd hoped. No kink, no research for his book, no other couple involved. Nothing but them, alone in his room at HUSH.

The cab pulled up at a building on a quiet residential street. May turned dreamily, then sat up and peered at the address, frowning and disoriented. This didn't look like HUSH.

"Where are we?"

"My place."

"Really?"

"You object?"

Oh, my God. She shook her head. "Not at all."

Not at *all.* Going back to the hotel would have been wonderful. But going to his place was taking their relationship to a new level, further away from fantasy, and more as if he wanted her in his life, as well as his bed.

And take that, Angie-who-took-six-months-to-find-out-where-he-lived.

She stopped her thoughts, ashamed of herself. *Whoa, Nellie.* One step at a time. But she couldn't help the giddy high that swept through her, building back dangerous hope.

The doorman greeted them, obviously surprised… and pleased…to see Beck. They rode the elevator to the sixth floor and emerged onto a landing with three apartments. Beck strode to the door on the left and inserted his key.

Okay, she admitted it, she was overwhelmed with lust for him, she was nearly overcome with feelings for him, but she was *dying* to see what his apartment looked like. Call it Pandora-like curiosity.

He opened the door and gestured her into a large-windowed living room with a view of Central Park on one side, and on another, a lit view of an onion-domed Russian Orthodox church across the street. The furniture was comfortable-looking, the art on the walls colorful and modern. A framed book cover—his first?—hung in a place of honor over an end table. The place had a welcoming feel—stylish without being overly decorated, and masculine without being all leather and bookcases.

Beck made the rounds, opening windows to dispel the stuffy unlived-in smell. Cool night air flowed into the small, neat kitchen, redone with granite counters and stainless steel appliances, into the room with a desk and computer that he must use as an office, and finally, into his bedroom where she followed, both eager and shy.

"I love your place."

"Thanks." He crossed to the park side of the room and lowered the blinds. "I've lived in this building for nearly ten years, though a few years ago I moved down here from a one-bedroom upstairs when I started getting decent royalty checks. The writing life is so uncertain, I didn't want to go hog wild with a giant mortgage in a more upscale neighborhood."

"Makes sense." She stood in the center of the room, soaking it all in. The hardwood floors, the oriental rugs, the blue, burgundy and cream patterned bedspread. And suddenly and painfully, she wanted the chance to know this room as intimately as he did.

Could she move here?

He came toward her and stood a foot away, hands on his hips. "You okay?"

She smiled bravely. "Very."

"Good. I wanted you to see this place so you'd know where I'd keep you if you decide to move. Separate bedrooms even, if you wanted."

He looked so disgusted by that idea that she giggled, ran her hands around and over his shoulders, his chest, his abdomen, and then had them meet for a party over the rapidly swelling bulge in his pants. "Or not separate."

"Much better idea." He took hold of the zipper at the base of her neck and inched it down, peeled the straps off her shoulders and watched the dress drop into a heap at her feet.

She stepped out of it, kicked off her flat shoes and stood quietly, feeling vulnerable and nervous, while his eyes made a leisurely exploration of her body in the white lace bra and matching panties.

"You are so beautiful." He moved close, lifted her breasts reverently in his palms. "A fantasy come to life."

She cringed. She didn't want to be a fantasy. She wanted—

"Stop that." His voice was the same sexy murmur; his hands warmed her skin on their way behind her; he undid her bra and slid it off.

"Stop what?" Her voice had dropped to a whisper; he was stroking her breasts, his hands warm in the cool breeze flowing through the room.

"Calling you a fantasy was a compliment. You're more real to me than any woman I've known."

She nodded, unable to speak. He stroked lower on her sides, hooked his thumbs in the soft cotton of her panties and took them down. Greedily, she unbuttoned his shirt and drew it off him, helped undo his pants and got him as naked as she was.

And oh, my gosh, talk about a fantasy come to life. His body was perfect, hard and male, not overlean or oversculpted. She could get used to seeing that every day, no question. Not to mention the man who came with it.

Could she move here?

He put his hands on her waist and slow-danced her over to his bed; she lay back on it, expecting him to join her, surprised when he didn't.

Instead, he stood at the foot, watching her. "You have no idea how amazing you look, naked on my bed."

May frowned. "Like a scene in your book?"

He grinned, the dimple deep in his cheek, prowled toward her across the mattress on his hands and knees like a stalking tiger and pounced, keeping his body off her with the strength in his arms. "Not from my book. This is all about us."

"Thank you." She stroked up the muscled columns of his arms; he whispered her name and looked down at her. Somehow she understood and opened her legs to him. *All about us.* He felt what she did.

He lowered himself slowly, controlling his descent, until he lay on top of her, his erection hot on her sex and abdomen.

Nothing in the world would ever feel as good as Beck Desmond naked against the length of her. She hooked her legs around his calves and her arms around his strong back and held on, savoring his warmth.

Could she move here?

How could she not?

He lifted slightly and began to move his penis across her clitoris; she slid her hands down to cup the muscles of his buttocks, to feel them bunch and lengthen, tense and release. She wanted to explore every part of him, enjoy the leisure they hadn't had until now.

He lifted farther, found her clitoris with his fingers. May stopped him. She didn't want foreplay, didn't care if she came or not, that wasn't what this was about, at least not for her. "I just want you."

"Are you sure?"

Her mouth spread into a smile, then widened into a grin. "Oh, yes. I'm sure."

He kissed her lingeringly, retrieved a condom from the drawer in his nightstand, pulled it on and moved over her again. She spread for him eagerly, wanting so badly to give him the pleasure he was obviously ready and hungry for.

Instead, he waited, rubbed his cheek against hers, and looked into her eyes with so much warmth she felt as if she'd start glowing from happiness.

"May."

"Yes." Her voice came out as low and husky as his.

"If you leave tomorrow you'll be taking part of me with you."

Then he slid inside her, and she lost herself to him, drawing him tight to her, answering his thrusts.

Time stopped; it was such a cliché, but she had no

idea how long they lay there, joined, making love, her heart so full she couldn't imagine this crazy infatuation could turn into anything but love.

He whispered her name and changed his rhythm, making circular motions with his hips, then back to the slow in-and-out, then changing again.

And out of the lovely peaceful glow of desire, a slow steady spark of excitement started to burn brighter. Urgency began to feed her movements; she struggled against his slow circles, her clitoris responding to the extra stimulation. Beck caught her mood and she sensed his own arousal climbing. His thrusts became harder, pulling out to the hilt, powerful surges back home, then slow, grinding circles again until the feverish high pitch of her excitement changed into certainty that she was going to come. The wave roared through her, twice as intense for what she carried in her heart.

And then the beauty of what they'd shared became too much, and she knew if she didn't act now, in another second she'd cry and tell him something May-ish like that she loved him, when this had all happened way too fast to be sure.

"Beck." She cried out in a hoarse voice, still coming down, clutching his shoulders. "Do it…harder. More."

He exhaled harshly and obeyed. She pulled her knees up; he pushed himself onto his arms and gave it to her, using the force of his lower body to drive his erection home, over and over until he suddenly tensed, his eyes closed, and she heard him breathe out a long thrilling "oh" of ecstasy.

Then his thrusts slowed, winding down though the last contractions, and he let himself relax gently on top of her.

One breath, two, three, and he lifted his head. Instead of a triumphant smile, he wore a serious, intense, almost anxious expression, mirroring exactly what she felt.

"May." He whispered her name, then paused, as if whatever he wanted to say was going to be difficult. "Nothing…I've experienced has come close to what has happened between us this week. And what just happened between us here."

She nodded, unable to speak.

He pulled carefully out of her, rolled to the side and drew her against him so her head fit comfortably under his chin and she could press her face against his skin. "You've said a few times that you're different with me. I'm different with you, too. I'm more thoughtful, considerate. I care deeply what you feel and think." He stopped for a full breath, and cleared his throat. "I guess I was a self-absorbed jerk before, God knows all my girlfriends tried to tell me. And probably my family, too."

She could say nothing. His voice rumbled through his chest and throat next to her ear, and his words were the most wonderful things she'd ever heard. This had to be love growing between them.

"I don't know how this happened. Especially to an old cold bastard like me, it's totally unexpected." He squeezed her close and kissed her hair. "And I'll tell you something else, May."

"Mmm?" She tipped her head back to see his eyes, which were light and earnest against his skin, and so beautiful it was almost painful.

"You're the first woman I've ever…"

I've ever loved. Loved. She waited, watching his struggle, trying to be patient, wanting to hear the word more than she wanted to go on living. Just that one, and she'd have what she needed to move here.

He kissed her, a slow, lingering sweet kiss that made her traitorous hopes soar like a let-go helium balloon.

"You're the first woman I've ever wanted this much."

MAY WOKE UP to the delicious sensation of warm, strong arms around her, and a warm, strong body at her back. Mmm. She'd love to wake up like this every day, in a glorious Beck cocoon.

Of course she could, the choice was still hers. But she'd been up during the night tossing and turning the problems and possible solutions over in her mind—and gotten nowhere.

After the power of what had happened between them last night, she knew she'd be a love-goner soon, if she wasn't already. But Beck? He wanted her, he'd shown it and said as much in many wonderful ways. Said she made him a better person, too—but so could a teacher or a parent or a good friend.

The truth was, moving halfway across the country after knowing someone four days—okay five now— was sheer insanity. If she and Beck didn't work out— and he sounded like in the past he'd changed women like he changed underwear—she'd have uprooted herself for nothing. And then what? Move back home with her tail between her legs? Take up her old life again? Somehow she had the feeling she wouldn't be able to go back. Not to Oshkosh, not if she'd been living in New York. Milwaukee, maybe, or Boston, or Denver. Or stay in New York without Beck and have a new life on her own. Which sounded lonely and frightening and not something May could handle.

On the other hand, maybe they would work out. Maybe the intensity of her emotions right now, this soon into the relationship was significant. Maybe she'd be happier with Beck than anyone she'd ever met or would ever meet. Didn't she owe it to herself to try?

She didn't know. And so her thoughts went round and round and up and down on the carousel of indecision, and please someone stop this crazy thing.

"Good morning." The warm cocoon at her back stirred, and a warm hand traveled down her bare arm, and over her hip, and to the front of her body where that hand did a few things that very quickly erased her need to angst over her future and replaced it with another one.

"Good morning to you." She wiggled onto her back, reached between them and found she was not dealing with that need all on her own. "Did you sleep well?"

"Pretty well." His very talented hand did other things that made it hard to concentrate on pleasuring him back. "You?"

"Pretty well."

"I was up for a few hours writing."

"Mmm, I remember the fun when you came back to bed. More revisions?"

"Yes, ma'am. But they're swimming along."

"Good."

She wanted to ask him if he'd discovered how to get Mack to fall in love. But that would be leading him to water and trying to force him to drink, and there was no way she'd do that to him.

Instead, she gave an exaggerated sigh and sped the rhythm of her hand on his erection. "I'm research again, huh."

"The best kind." He leaned over and kissed her neck, making tiny lazy circles with his tongue.

"Do you need to write more today?"

"Yes. But I'd rather spend the day in bed with you." Her grip tightened on his penis. "Do you want to work right now?"

"Hmm." He thrust up into her hand. "Not, um…not really *right* now."

She giggled and sat up, straddled him and rubbed her sex back and forth over his erection. "Are you sure?"

He grabbed her hips, settled her more firmly and rocked against her. "I'm quite, *quite* sure."

"Because I'm happy to leave now, and let you work."

"No." He fumbled for another condom from his nightstand. "No, seriously, you're not bothering me."

"I'm not?" She leaned forward and scraped her teeth over his nipple, followed it with a long, slow exploration using her tongue.

"No." He breathed the word out, eyes blissfully closed and May felt a sudden and glorious burst of female power and tenderness.

Could she go home to Oshkosh and risk never feeling this way again? Risk not finding out if this could turn into love for both of them? Risk on both sides of the equation. May didn't have a lot of experience with risk.

She took the condom from his hand and tore open the packet. Rolled the latex over his erection and slowly lowered herself onto him. Rode him using her hips, the strength in her thighs and in her arms to keep herself braced and in motion.

He moaned, closed his eyes; his lips parted in something close to a snarl; he looked so fierce, so wild, so carried away by the pleasure she was giving him, she had an absurd desire to stop right there, and sketch him. So she could carry the picture of him with her always. A picture of what they were together, of what he was to her and what he'd made her into. A picture of freedom, power, indulgent sexuality. And love? Maybe even love.

Her thighs worked harder, up and down; he moved his hand from her hip to between her legs, to stimulate her clitoris while she rode him. She moaned and moved faster, caught by arousal and sent to a higher place of passion where nothing mattered but their joining, their connection; her desire to pleasure him, as strong as her own need to climax.

She hit her peak seconds before his, felt it tearing into her, through her, then subsiding gently into total and unapologetic bliss.

How could she ever bring herself to leave him?

She melted down onto his chest, felt his arms come around her and squeeze tightly before relaxing into a comfortable hold. They lay together in silence. What was he thinking? What was he feeling? Why didn't she feel bold enough to ask?

Because in spite of what had just passed between them, she couldn't quite quell the fear that instead of "I love you, don't leave me," he was thinking of how to portray Mack. Or what he was going to have for breakfast. Or how his fourteen other girlfriends must be getting impatient for his call.

His chest expanded under her cheek, then contracted in a long sigh.

"*Now* do you have to work?" She lifted her head and smiled at the resigned look on his face. "Yes. You do."

"I'm sorry. I have to turn this in today before my agent leaves on—"

"Shh." She put her finger to his lips. "It's fine. You need to write."

"And you need to get back to Hush and pack."

Her face fell, she couldn't help it. "Right."

"So you can move your stuff here until you find a place to live." He pushed her hair back from her face, grinning wickedly. She laughed and moved off him, hating to break the connection, wishing she could just say yes and be done with it.

Was this the last time they'd make love or the first of many? Would she go back to her room, pack, check out and head for the airport? Or go back to her room, pack, check out and head directly back here, or to stay with Clarissa?

She didn't know, couldn't decide, this was so unlike her. Usually she knew instinctively what to do, which path she wanted to take. The problem this time was that May from Oshkosh was having an all-out war with Veronica of New York, and neither seemed able either to conquer or surrender.

"What's keeping you from deciding, May?"

"Multiple personality disorder." She lay next to him. "Me in Oshkosh versus me in New York."

He laughed deep in his chest and pulled her to him. "Okay. What is there back in Oshkosh that you can't leave?"

Good question. Was it just the security of sameness? "A job."

"As much fun as Clarissa's here?"

She made a face and shook her head. "And family."

"That's what airplanes are for." His smile faded and

disappeared. "What about this guy you were seeing? Is he part of the hesitation?"

A picture of Dan rose in her mind. Laughing, swaggering, tender, serious. She loved Dan. In a quiet, sure and steady way. Nothing like the wild, passionate feelings she had for Beck.

So which feelings were more real?

"I don't know. Maybe. Which is stupid, since he broke up with me."

"Will you stop beating yourself up?" He grabbed her hand and mimed her pummeling herself. "Emotions are too seldom rational. But I can say, regardless of my personal stake, that if he made you feel anything less than dazzling and exciting and amazing, you shouldn't go back to him."

She nodded, while part of her registered that no one could be dazzling and exciting and amazing forever. "You may be right."

"So you'll stay?" He looked so eager she laughed.

"Maybe I should go home for a while, for a cooling-off period and see how far we cool."

"Cool?" He looked at her as if she had suggested ritual sacrifice. "You were in bed with me all night long and think there's a chance of that?"

She wrinkled her nose. "I guess not."

"We wouldn't cool. If anything we'd heat further."

He was right. Her idea had been a gray attempt at a black-and-white solution. Either she went home and made peace with that decision, or she moved here and took the risk. She couldn't have it both ways, and the guarantee she so desperately wanted, that she and Beck would work out forever, wasn't going to magically materialize in the next few hours.

So.

"I need to make the final decision out of your arousing and magnetic presence, Mr. Desmond." She sat up and swung her legs off the bed. "And you need to work anyway."

"True." He sighed regretfully and drew a warm hand down the length of her spine. "I'll call down to Mark, our morning doorman, and ask him to get you a cab. What time is this flight you're not taking?"

She laughed. "Five-thirty."

"I'll come meet you at the hotel for lunch. Will you let me take you to the airport if you decide to go?"

"I'd love that." She stood up and found her clothes, put them on, feeling rumpled and sad and complicated, looking forward to a shower, or maybe a nice long soak in the whirlpool tub when she got back to her room.

Her last shoe had just slipped on when Mark called up that her cab was waiting.

The end of the adventure or the beginning? She kissed Beck at his apartment door, insisted she could find her way and let herself out into the early-morning sunshine and rapidly warming July air.

Would she be back here? Maybe soon? Take the risk and plunge into a totally new life?

She hauled her cell out of her purse and dialed.

"Ginny, it's May."

"May, it's early, what is up? You don't sound happy."

"I am and I'm not."

She brought her friend up to date, Beck, Clarissa, Beck, dinner out, Beck, Beck's family, Beck, Beck, Beck...

"So now I don't know what to do."

"Yes you do."

"I do?" Her voice cracked hopefully.

"Hello? You're in love with him, May. And he's madly in love with you."

"But Angie—"

"Screw Angie, she's just bitter. Now listen, because I know what I'm talking about. This is the real thing, honey. You go to lunch with him today, you tell him you'll stay in New York and move in with him, or Aunty Ginny will come down there and kick your ass."

May giggled, slightly hysterically. "I don't even know if—"

"*When* he hears this news, he will drop to his knees, tell you he loves you and ask you to marry him and have his babies. If not this afternoon, then soon."

"And you know this how?"

"He's given you all the signs you need, May." Her bubbly voice grew uncharacteristically serious. "He took you to meet his parents, he took you to his place even though whatsername said he never would. He cares, he loves you, he shows it in everything he does. But the guy has his pride. He needs something from you now. And it's something you want to give him."

"Oh, gosh. Ginny." She started to cry and fumbled for a tissue. "You're right."

"Of *course* I'm right." She chuckled. "I'm really happy for you. You deserve this. Now call me when it's over and tell me how big the ring is."

May laughed through her tears, said a heartfelt thanks and signed off. Bless Ginny's romantic soul. Of course May knew what she wanted. She just needed one last push to overcome her fear.

The cab dropped her at the hotel. She paid, tipping generously, and allowed hunky HUSH employees to escort her out of the cab, into the lobby…

Where in one of the black art deco chairs, looking exhausted and unshaven, with Eartha Kitty firmly planted in his lap...sat Dan.

12

MAY FROZE, right there in the lobby. Dan had come for her. To take her back to Wisconsin. Exactly as her father had come after her mom when he knew she'd had enough adventure. When he knew she was moving slowly and surely ahead to a life of unhappiness in a place she wasn't suited for.

The fantasy bubble of moving to New York and marrying Beck popped and showered all over the carpet at her feet. Dan looked so dear and familiar, miserably uncomfortable and out of place sitting there, her heart nearly broke. How could she have been planning to give up on all the years they'd had together?

Her first instinct was to run and throw herself into his arms. But in the next instant, she remembered that while her back had been turned in Wisconsin, he'd been lying on his, whupping it up with D-Cup Charlene, and she found it suddenly much easier not to.

She approached slowly instead, shaky from rioting emotions. Dan and Eartha Kitty looked up and saw her at the exact same time. Eartha gave her a brief, green "back off" look and gazed imploringly up at Dan, who'd stopped scratching her ears when he saw May. In fact he'd stopped moving altogether.

Uh-oh. She must have a huge With Someone Else Last Night sign tacked to her forehead.

Eartha gave an annoyed meow, finding herself on the way to the floor as Dan stood up slowly, still staring at May. He looked terrible, as if he hadn't slept in days. Black stubble covered his cheeks and chin and dark circles shadowed his even darker eyes. She fought bravely not to feel maternal and tender, and won. Almost.

He strode toward her, nearly tripping over Eartha, still trying to rub against his legs. So guess what. Even the aloof and distant Eartha needed love.

"Where have you been, May? I've been here all night."

"In the *lobby?*" She gaped at him in horror, guilt crowding her chest. "All *night?*"

He nodded and stood, hands on his hips, looking anxious and angry. "You weren't here. I didn't know where else to go. I kept thinking you had to come back soon—and I wasn't going to pay for a room at these prices."

"No." She sighed and gestured toward the elevators. Dan wouldn't even pay full price for a box of cereal. "Let's go to my room where we can talk."

They got on the elevator with another couple and stood in excruciating silence until the fourteenth floor delivered them from elevator hell. To call May conflicted was like calling Niagara Falls a rivulet. Dan? Beck? Stay? Move home?

"This is us." May made her way to what was supposed to be her and Trevor's room, leading her one and only boyfriend, Dan, after having just spent the night with Beck.

No. Dull and predictable she wasn't. Not anymore. And maybe not ever again. Though a little less weirdness would be nice.

"So." Her key card unlocked the door and she motioned Dan inside. "Welcome to Hush."

He gave her a look she deserved. "Yeah, thanks."

She walked after him into the room, where he'd turned to stone, fists at his sides, staring at the bed. May rolled her eyes. Yes, Dan, it was a bed. Hotel rooms generally had them. And yes, she'd been doing exactly what he'd been doing with buxom Whatsername. So get over it.

Her next step brought her around him so his body no longer obstructed her view.

Holy moly. She followed a gasp with a burst of raucous laughter. Oh, this could *not* get any more bizarre. On the bed stood what was undoubtedly Trevor's traditional farewell. A much larger-than-life chocolate phallus, complete with large and detailed chocolate testicles. The whole thing was wrapped in iridescent cellophane, and stuck straight up into the air like a rocket about to take off and crash a hole through the ceiling.

May glanced at Dan's rigid back and managed to get her laughter under control. "Well, isn't that a lovely item."

Dan swung around, not remotely amused. "Who is that…thing from?"

She advanced coolly around the bed and picked up the card nestled at the base of the atrocity. "Probably Trevor."

"*Who* is Trevor?"

She opened the note.

Thanks for the best week of my life. Here's a little—or rather big—something to remember me by. Let's do it again, soon.
Trevor.

Oh, how special. She put the card back into the envelope, trying her best not to giggle again. Dan deserved more than that. "Trevor is the guy I was supposed to meet here."

"Supposed to?" His voice cracked hopefully.

"Turned out he had an unavoidable engagement with his wife."

"He was *married?*"

"I didn't know."

"So what the hell are you doing here now?"

She tossed the card into the trash and finally faced him. "I was going to ask you the same thing."

"I've come to take you home. And to apologize for being such an ass. I've been waiting all night for you to come back from…wherever you were." His set jaw clearly indicated he was due an explanation.

"I was at Beck Desmond's condo."

"Beck Desmond?" His face contorted in disbelief. "The writer?"

She nodded and kicked off her shoes, started to peel off her stockings. "We spent a lot of the week together."

He laughed nervously. "Come on, May."

"What?" She tossed her stockings onto the desk chair and regarded him calmly. Of course he wouldn't believe her. Any more than she'd believe him if he said he'd spent the week with Cameron Diaz.

"Beck Desmond?"

"He's been staying at Hush researching a novel."

"And you spent the week with him."

"Yes."

"In what capacity?"

"I'd guess very similar to what you were doing with Charlene."

His face darkened; he strode around the bed and

stood close to her, searching her face as if he still held out hope the May he knew was in there somewhere.

"Okay." His face gentled; he drew his fingers over his temples and down his jaw in a gesture she knew as well as she knew her own name. "I can't get angry at you. I understand what you were doing. I was doing the same thing."

"What?"

"Looking for something more than you and I had. Going after something that seemed bright and shiny and new and exciting." He took her shoulders, leaned forward and kissed her, a warm familiar kiss. "But it's not real, May. It's fantasy, it's the greener grass next door."

Sick panic invaded May's stomach. Wasn't this what she was so afraid of? Would she move here and find down the road that she and Beck had stagnated into routine and compromise that satisfied neither of them, same as she and Dan had?

"Charlene wasn't what I wanted. You are." His voice dropped to the soothing baritone that had unerringly made her feel the world was okay. Now it made her anxious, confused.

He found the tight spot that always sat at the base of her neck and started massaging. "I had to learn the hard way, and I'm sorry for what I must have put you through to make you come to a place like…this."

May gave her surroundings the once-over. "Uh, Dan, this isn't exactly Sing-Sing."

"You know what I mean."

She stared, frowning, into the eyes that were staring back into hers. Dark beautiful brown eyes that used to send firecrackers shooting along her spine. She was supposed to say, *Yes, Dan, of course I know what you mean.* But the new May wanted to hear him spell it out. "I'm not sure I do."

He looked startled. Hadn't she ever challenged him? "You don't belong in a hotel like this."

"Why not?"

"May…" His hands tightened on her shoulders and she got the impression he wanted to shake her.

"Let's hear it, Dan. What is it? I'm not sexual enough? I'm not sophisticated enough? I'm not trampy enough?"

"Yes."

"Yes?"

"All of the above. You don't belong here, May. You belong home in Oshkosh with me. If you want more excitement—obviously we both do—then we need to find a way to make it happen there, between us."

She gritted her teeth. He was right. Wasn't he? Didn't every relationship deserve to be worked on? How rare was it to find someone like Dan, who fit her so well? What did she know about Beck? Not enough to change her life for him. Not nearly enough. Dan loved her. Beck…Beck said he wanted her.

"Pack now." Dan kissed her again, on her nose, which always made her feel like a little girl. "We can talk more about this on the plane."

May pulled away. Pack now? He sounded like her father. Why weren't they discussing this? He wasn't even taking her seriously, hadn't asked her how she felt, why she came here, what she'd learned. "My flight's not until five-thirty and—"

"There's standby room on mine."

"—I'm considering staying in New York."

His confident smile faded from his lips as what she'd said sunk in. "Staying? As in another week's vacation?"

She shook her head. "Moving."

"What?" He took a deep breath. "Because of this Beck person?"

A nod, this one tentative and guilty, which he'd notice and pounce on.

"Be serious, May. Unless you met him in Oshkosh and were seeing him there…" He paused and waited for May to shake her head in denial. "You've known this guy for four days. *Four days.* How many other women do you think a guy like that has?"

Her stomach flipped. "None."

"What, you think he'd admit it? You think celebrity authors fall in love in four days? Sure they do. A *different woman* every four days. Come on, May, get real. You're in way over your head here."

Oh, God. He had her. He'd found her darkest fear and was exploiting it mercilessly. Unfortunately, he also had a really good chance of being right. "It's not like that."

"Oh, right. Let me guess. He told you he'd never felt like this before."

She flinched; she couldn't help it. Dan saw the flinch. An in a moment of horror, she realized he'd use that, too. She started feeling the same desperate panic she felt every time they argued like this. As if everything she believed and felt and knew to be true was being slowly and systematically taken from her.

"Has he told you he loves you?"

"No…."

"So you're going to change your entire life for some guy who's good in bed?"

"It's more than that." She heard her own voice. Shrill and afraid, like a teenager insisting the quarterback wanted her in the back of his car to discuss philosophy.

"May…" Dan pulled her against him, and she let herself be cradled in his warmth and steady strength. "Don't you see what you're doing?"

"What am I doing?" Why was she asking him? Didn't she know herself?

"You're trying to be like your mother. You're going after something thrilling that doesn't exist. I'm here. I'm real. I'm like your father, I want you to stop reaching for something you're not, something that isn't going to make you happy. This guy will eat you alive and spit you out in pieces. I don't want you to be hurt."

A flash memory of sobbing alone in her apartment night after night did an effective job of extracting her brain from the enticing pull of his comfort and security. "Except by you?"

His body tensed; score one for team Ellison.

"I don't know what I was thinking, May. I woke up one day and felt too young to have everything planned out until I died. It was stupid guy freakout stuff." He put his hands to her temples and lifted her face toward him, his dark eyes clear and honest and uncomplicated. "I'll live with the regret of what I did to you the rest of my life. But I can bear that as long as you're there with me. So I can make it up to you every day for the rest of your life. I need you, May. I love you."

His voice was thick, emotional, humble and utterly sincere. He loved her. He'd made a mistake. He regretted it. He was willing to move ahead with her. Wasn't that what she'd wanted all along? If she went with Beck, would she someday come back to Dan just like this, hoping he'd forgive her stupidity?

"You don't belong in this city, May. You can't handle this pace of life, this kind of stress. You aren't cut out for it."

You don't. You can't. You aren't. Suddenly she heard Beck's voice and Clarissa's. They'd both warned her against Dan keeping her down.

He hadn't once asked her what she was feeling. What she wanted and why. He was telling her what she felt. Telling her what she was going to do. Telling her about her life, about Beck and about himself. Making her feel small and helpless and dull.

"You belong with me, May." Somehow his grandmother's locket was in his hands; he was putting it over her head, where it felt heavy and unfamiliar after so many months without it. "I know that as surely as I know you still love me."

Another kiss; she tasted tears—hers or his? The kiss was long, passionate, and it hit May with out-of-the-blue certainty that she was saying goodbye.

She'd come too close to dutifully going back to believing every word he said. Maybe Dan was right about Beck, and Angie, too, maybe May was naive. Time would tell. But she sure as hell wasn't going back to more of this.

May Hope Ellison was moving to New York. Not for Beck. Not to get away from Dan. For herself. For the person she thought she could become here. For the person she already was.

She opened her mouth to speak; he laid a finger across her lips. "I know what you're thinking, feeling. You don't even have to tell me. I know you that well, May."

"Oh, Dan." She took off the necklace, laid it carefully on the bed, took his face in her hands and kissed his forehead, tenderly, sweetly, as if he was her favorite son. "I'm so sorry. But I don't think you know me at all."

DONE. Beck stretched his cramped shoulder and neck muscles and glanced over at the clock. Nearly lunch-time. May had left around seven and he'd been work-ing like a fiend for nearly five hours. Usually he needed a break after two or three.

He got up from his chair—damn shame his favorite was at HUSH—and stretched, working his neck around a few more times. He needed to fax the last revised pages to Alex, and then call May and make arrangements for lunch.

And, he hoped, the rest of his life. Or hell, one thing at a time, at least the next year or so.

He collected the spewed-out stack of paper from the printer, loaded it into his fax machine, dialed Alex's of-fice number and punched Send as if he were slamming home the winning slot-machine quarter.

Hallelujah. Done. Now to wait for Alex's reaction.

Amazing the difference from the first draft to the re-vised version. He'd rewritten—well there was so much to change, he'd practically started from scratch—the love scene between Mack and his heroine…Hope. Beck grinned at the name. Hope, not surprisingly, had turned out to be a woman with an old-fashioned sweet exterior and a sensual wild core that would keep Mack coming back for the rest of his literary life.

In the first draft, sex had been for Mack what it had always been for Beck. Erotic and extremely pleasurable. From his current perspective, that early version felt flat, emotionless—and dare he quote a fascinating woman he knew, "dull and predictable."

The new scene was simply a reflection of everything he'd been feeling last night. Sex with May had been a big wake-up slap in the face, as a writer and as a man.

How could he have thought falling in love could

make Mack less masculine? Beck fairly roared with testosterone this morning. Could hardly restrain himself from beating his chest and giving a few Tarzan yodels.

The only thing holding him back, besides disturbing the neighbors, was the fear that May would choose to go back to Wisconsin. That five days wouldn't be enough to convince her she was selling herself short. That the safety of this Dan person—whom Beck would frankly like to sock in the nose—would beckon, and the risk of moving here would seem too great.

Of course it was a risk. A huge one. In her position… No. In her position, feeling the way he felt, he'd jump. Because this week had been like emerging from a cocoon of routine and emotional suppression, and spreading his mighty butterfly wings. He felt like calling each of his old girlfriends and apologizing. Every one of their complaints now made sense. May had not only shown him what they'd been missing, but proved to him he could provide it all to the right woman. That he was capable of falling in love.

Last night, "I love you" had been welling up in him so strongly he still couldn't believe he hadn't said it. But the fear, the vulnerability…yeah, okay, so he was still a guy. Instead, he'd showed her as many other ways and with as many other words as he could manage.

As for the future—he was pretty sure she felt more for him than a chemical pull. And after last night, meeting his family, and that intense passionate experience in bed, she had to know he felt a hell of a lot more than that. But she was such a fascinating mixture, a work in progress, emerging from a cocoon of her own. If she was just now discovering this new bolder more erotic side of herself, she might not be willing to be tied down into love. She might want to explore it more fully, back with Dan or with other men—

He tossed the rest of his water into the sink and slammed the glass down so hard on the granite counter, he was surprised it didn't break.

Do not think about that.

He strode back into his bedroom, dialed HUSH on his cell, to keep his landline free for Alex's call, and asked for May's room.

"Oh. Hi."

He tensed. The nerves in her voice, the awkward way she spoke… She was going home.

"Hi, May. I'm almost done here, I'm waiting for my agent to read the pages." Fear made his own voice flat. "Are you nearly ready for lunch?"

"Oh. Well…"

He sank onto his bed, dreading whatever was coming.

"What's up, May?" The words came out calmly and quietly, somehow he managed that much.

"Dan's here."

Dan. Rage poured into Beck's body, made his gut and fist clench. Dan was here. To take her back, like the fairy tale May clung to of her father "rescuing" her mom from a life she wasn't meant to live. To conk her over the head, dump her into a sack, hoist her over his shoulder and make sure she lived a life of stifled submission chained to his side.

"Would he like to join us?" Sarcasm cut into his tone and he told himself to calm the hell down and let her talk.

She giggled and his heart rose. "Somehow I don't think so."

Okay. Giggles were better than icy politeness. But

she still wasn't telling him anything he wanted to hear. "What's the story, May? What does this mean?"

"Beck...I...this is sort of awkward..."

"Right." He closed his eyes, took a deep breath, trying not to imagine them in bed together so he wouldn't go over there and put his fist through Dan's face. "Are we still on for lunch?"

"I don't know if...hang on." He heard her muffled speech and a deep answering voice. The idea of another man in a room with her that had a bed, even if they'd done nothing on it but sit and talk, was driving him out of his mind.

"I'd like to see you." Her voice came back on the line, softer, as if she'd sent Dan away but was still afraid of being overheard. "But he's here now..."

His phone started ringing. Damn. That would be Alex with her reaction to his pages; he had to talk to her today, she was leaving early for the weekend. "May, I have to take this call from my agent. Can I call you back in a while?"

"Yes. Okay." She sounded breathless, overwhelmed; he said goodbye and pounced on the call from Alex, feeling more protective and more scared than he'd ever felt in his life. "Hello?"

"Damn, you are a genius."

He closed his eyes in relief. The need for more revisions today would not be welcome, to put it mildly.

"Beck, this scene rocks. It's tender, sexy, passionate and, oh, my God, the emotions in it are enough to make this middle-aged woman melt. I'm serious, where have you been hiding this stuff?"

"It's new for me."

"You met someone, didn't you?"

His jaw clenched. This would be a rare personal admission from him; he liked to keep his professional relationships strictly professional. "Yeah."

"Ha! I knew you'd fall eventually, congratulations. Well, your writing thanks you, I thank you, your editor will thank you, and the reading public will kneel and worship you."

He winced and managed a smile. "Thanks are enough."

"These lines are great. The ending is perfect. I love it especially when Mack wants to tell Hope he loves her and he doesn't. That was brilliant. Keep her guessing. Keep the readers waiting."

He frowned. "Keep her guessing? That's how it comes across?"

"Sure, and that's what I love about it. That's what keeps Mack tough and on top."

Beck stood abruptly and caught a faint reflection of himself in the glass over a Monet print. "You don't think she knows he loves her?"

Alex made a sound of incredulity. "How? Because he screws her more than once?"

He turned away from himself and started pacing. "But he tells her he's never felt this way before, he asks her to stay in New York, and—"

"You've never dated any men, have you, Beck."

"Uh." He raised his eyebrows. "That would be no."

"You wouldn't believe what women have to put up with. All the crap we hear. It's all designed either to get into our pants, get into our pants again or get into our pants the next time. And sometimes to keep us from buying murder weapons. But you can't fake an 'I love you.' I've never met the man yet who would risk messing with that kind of power."

Beck stopped pacing. One of his mighty butterfly wings was apparently still stuck in the cocoon of male cluelessness.

He needed to get to HUSH. Now. "So it's all good?"

"It's all good, baby. You're going to make it huge with this book. Have you thought about what will happen in the next one? You want Mack and Hope to break up? You want to kill Hope off and have Mack mourn her deeply while screwing random babes?"

He grinned wickedly. "I think they should get married, have babies and start saving for private school tuition and retirement."

"Oh, my God. She's got you bad. Okay, we'll talk about that another time. Have a great weekend, and thanks, these changes are perfect."

"My pleasure." He punched off the phone and made a beeline for his front door. To hell with Mack. To hell with Dan. He and May belonged together. He loved her.

And whatever she ended up deciding—he was going to make damn well sure she knew it.

13

MAY TOOK ANOTHER dutiful bite of what was undoubtedly a delicious turkey sandwich on olive foccaccia bread, but she couldn't taste a thing. Opposite her, at the table in her room that had held flowers from Trevor her first day here a million years ago, sat Dan, glowering at his fancy sandwich, clearly longing for ham and American cheese on white with extra mayo. She'd given up on lunch with Beck when the clock ticked later and later and poor Dan admitted he was fainting from hunger. He probably hadn't eaten since he'd arrived last night.

So here they sat. Dan hadn't wanted to leave the hotel to eat, he'd said one trip over from the airport and one trip back through this horrible town was enough for him. From there they'd gone back to how could she possibly think she wanted to move to a city like this? There was no room to breathe. Nothing growing that hadn't been planted. The noise, the stress, the crowds, the pollution, the litter—

She'd survived his tirade and his denial by thinking of the roof garden upstairs, would it become hers? She'd love it to. Her patch of green, her nature connection during the warm months in New York. And hey, there was another point in favor of her decision to move here, there were more warm months in New York than Wisconsin.

And of course, she was thinking of Beck…who hadn't called back yet. Why not? Was he really taking this long to talk to his agent, over forty-five minutes?

She chided herself. Of course he was. Dan's words had made her uneasy, given her a desperate need for more reassurance from Beck that she wasn't just his latest Lego woman conquest. But sure, he could be having a long talk. What did she know about publishing?

She just wanted him here, to share her news with him, even if he didn't fulfill her fantasy on his knees with the promise of eternity. And if nothing else, a break from this stress would be nice. She and Dan had talked—okay, argued—all morning, except for the few minutes she'd stolen to shower. And even then, she'd been acting partly out of irrational guilt talking to Dan with Beck's scent still on her body.

Mr. Oshkosh couldn't—or wouldn't—accept her decision. He knew what was good for her. He wasn't impressed by any of her reasoning. He couldn't tune in to her attempts to share her experiences and feelings. How different from talking with Beck.

Dan took a long drink of milk and she watched the familiar ripples of his throat swallowing it down. Tears threatened her own throat and she took a slow calming breath. Leaving something old and dear and safe, on the verge of something new and scary and—God, she hoped—wonderful gave her the strength to see this through.

He put the glass down and caught her watching him, which made her rummage through her brain to fill the silence. "So, what time do you think you should leave?"

She winced at the pain in his eyes. She hadn't meant to sound so eager…

"I'd like to shower, then I'll go." He spoke quietly, and the sad weight in her stomach grew heavier.

"Okay." What else was there to say? He thought she'd be back; she knew she wouldn't be—at least not for more than the time it took to settle her affairs in Wisconsin and return here. If New York and Beck didn't work, then somewhere else would. But not Oshkosh, not now, not until she did some further exploring of who she was and what she could accomplish. After that, who knew? Maybe she'd decide Oshkosh was the best place for her after all. Maybe she'd get tired of big-city bustle and want to go back. Maybe when kids came.

Just not now.

Dan went into the bathroom and closed the door. The shower came on, and she wandered to the window, drew back the curtains and gazed up at the blue sky and the thin clouds accumulating overhead. Then down at the street, teeming with energy and life. New York, New York, a helluva town. She hated being stuck here in the room; she wanted nothing more than to be out in all of it, taking it on one step at a time.

Okay, there was one thing she wanted more than to be out. She turned to gaze longingly at the phone, as if longing badly enough would make it ring. He said he'd call…

Instead of the phone coming to life, the shower stopped, and a knock sounded on the door. She sighed and walked over to answer. After the chocolate erection, if Trevor had anything else to give, she didn't want to know what it—

"Hi."

"Hi." Her voice came out breathless and gooey.

Beck. So much better than a chocolate erection.

She stood there inanely, staring up into his warm

blue-gray eyes and bang, it hit her. She loved him. Truly, deeply and always. And since she was May, truly-deeply-always brought another layer of fear and vulnerability to her already overlayered morning.

But then…a man who was ready to move on to next week's sweet thing couldn't stand there and gaze that adoringly at this week's, could he?

God, she hoped not. "Come in."

"Is Dan still here?"

"Yes." Dan's voice came out of the bathroom.

May winced and mouthed "Sorry."

Beck nodded. His hands went to his hips; the warmth in his eyes faded to wariness.

Dan chose that moment to come out of the bathroom wearing only a towel, his stocky chest covered in damp hair.

"You must be Beck Desmond." He extended his hand for a shake, smiling at the taller man, confident and appearing relaxed to anyone who didn't know that his lips weren't usually that thin. Everything about the moment was calculated to communicate one thing: Back off, she's had fun with you this week but she's mine and I just gave her and the bed a workout to prove it.

Beck's eyes narrowed, then shot to May's. He didn't shake Dan's hand.

"No." She put her hand up like a traffic cop, to keep Beck from fitting any more apparent pieces together. "Don't even go there. He spent the night in the lobby and needed to clean up. We've been talking all morning, that's it."

"I'm here to take her home."

Beck gave Dan a look that would reduce anyone less stubborn to ashes. "Is that what she wants?"

He nodded. "She doesn't know it yet, but it is."

Beck's lips curved into a slow smile. "She doesn't, huh."

"No." Dan's neck started to turn red; his ears followed suit as he realized what he sounded like. "I'm trying to save her pain in the long run. She's in too deep here. She doesn't belong in New York. And she doesn't belong with you."

"She said that?"

He flushed deeper. "She doesn't realize it yet. But she will."

Beck turned bitterly amused eyes to May. "Is that right, May?"

"I…" she felt her face turn as scarlet as Dan's ears. She desperately wanted to believe she belonged with Beck. But how the hell did she know? She loved him…but he'd only said he wanted her.

"You'll break her heart."

"Ah. So, Dan, you are not only the keeper of everything May is feeling, but everything I am, too. Is that right?"

"All I'm saying is that you have the wrong idea about her."

Beck folded his arms across his chest. "I do."

"This—" Dan's gesture encompassed the hotel, the city, the whole week "—was all a reaction to breaking up with me."

May cringed. All about him. How could she not have seen this for so many years?

"She's trying to be something she's not because I said something stupid that had more to do with me than her."

I. I. Me. Me. Of course. More to do with him.

Enough. She wouldn't let his words color her feelings

anymore. She was figuratively putting her hands over her ears and chanting, *lalalalala*. Whatever was between her and Beck would be discovered alone between her and Beck and was no longer subject to Dan's interpretation.

"That fake version of her is the woman you're into." Dan gestured toward May in frustration. "She can't keep up that front forever. And guys like you—"

Beck held up a hand to stop him. Amazingly, it worked. "Strange as it might sound to you, Dan, I'd like to hear what May has to say about all this. And for the record, 'guys like you' are in no position to judge 'guys like me' since you know nothing about me."

The men glared at each other, then simultaneously turned to look at May, Dan defensive and stiff, Beck encouraging but cautious.

May got to her feet, unutterably weary. This was like starring in her very own Molière farce, only it wasn't turning out to be funny. "Dan, I think you should go catch your plane."

Dan stared at her in mute frustration, then grabbed clothes from his overnight bag and disappeared into the bathroom, leaving Beck and May gazing at each other in a painful silence. So much to say to each other…and all of it overheard if they tried to talk now.

Dan banged out, fully dressed, crammed his dirty clothes into his case and hoisted it to his shoulder. "I'll be in Milwaukee to meet the five-thirty flight, May."

She sighed. Whatever. He could cool his stubborn heels there forever if it suited him. "Have a good flight, Dan."

"Right." The word dripped with the scorn of a man who understood things his dimwitted ex-girlfriend never would. And in that moment, May saw him for the lost, limited, sweet man he was and felt sad and sorry for him. And damn grateful to Charlene's breasts for luring him away and making her escape possible.

Dan grabbed her to him, kissed her roughly and banged out of the room. Exit stage left. And goodbye.

May eyed Beck, who eyed her back, and the weight of what had just been said and what needed to be said pressed so heavily she couldn't say anything at all.

Beck pointed to the bed. "Nice chocolate penis."

May burst out laughing, covered her mouth with her hands and laughed some more, ignoring the tears that mixed into it.

Arms came around her and she giggled and hiccupped unattractively as the last of the laughter tumbled through her, as she leaned into his sympathetic supportive warmth, closing her eyes, knowing she'd made the right decision to stay, and hoping he felt for her even part of what she felt for him.

"Are you dying to get out of here as much as I am?"

She smiled up at him through tears and probably flowing mascara. "More."

"Let's go."

"Where?"

"For a walk?"

"Sounds wonderful."

They descended into the lobby and left the cool, perfectly controlled peace for the warm, breezy, exhilarating chaos that was New York. Up Madison Avenue, past an oddly stumbling man loudly lamenting the plight of the housefly, past rushing executives, strolling tourists, moms with strollers, west on 42nd past the majestic public library building and the eight-acre green of Bryant Park behind it. Up Sixth Avenue, where the grass, trees and sunshine of Central Park beckoned ahead, waiting to be explored.

May clung to Beck's hand, happy to let the conversation wander as casually as their feet. They talked about his book, about his agent, about buildings they were passing. When the moment was right, they'd talk out what really mattered, and May knew she'd be heard.

"Rockefeller Center is over there." He gestured across the street.

"Is that where they have the tree at Christmas and the skating rink?"

"On Fifth Avenue, yes. I've been to the lighting ceremony every year." His hand on hers tightened. "Would you like to go with me in December?"

Even though his tone was light and teasing, she felt his tension and heard the question he really wanted answered.

A smile there was no way she could deny spread her mouth, and laughter impossible to quell bubbled up in her throat. "I would love to."

Beck stopped, pulled her around so she was up against his chest, and walked her back toward the building behind her so they'd be out of the pedestrian route. "You'll fly in from Wisconsin?"

She shook her head, let all the love she was feeling shine in her eyes. "I'll call you from my posh New York City pad and say hey, let's go, babe. Meet you at your place in half an hour."

"Really?" He was gazing at her so intently and so seriously the laughter went out of her.

"If it's what you want…"

"May." He rolled his eyes. "I'm not Dan, what do *you* want?"

"You." She said the word, then inhaled as long and slowly and carefully as she could, reminding herself she was doing this for her, and that if he didn't want her as much or as long as she wanted him, it wouldn't be the end of her. This was all a big beautiful beginning.

But of course some little sentence that implied commitment would be nice, too.

Instead, he did something almost as good, which was to say her name and kiss her with such joy and passion and what seemed like relief, that she knew in her soul there would be no new sweet young thing next week, or the week after, or the week after that….

That would do. That was enough after five days. She couldn't expect—

"I love you."

A car honked; pedestrians passed. How could they when the world had just stopped?

"Beck." His name burst out on a sob of laughter. Tears came into her eyes and she blinked stupidly through them, grinning like mad, sure she looked and sounded like a woman possessed, sure neither of them cared. "I love you, too."

He cupped the back of her neck, let his thumbs trace her cheekbones. "I didn't think love could happen in five days. Hell, I didn't think love could happen for me at all. But it has. You're the most amazing woman I've—"

"No, no, I'm boring, timid, dull, predictable…"

"Oh, right, I forgot." He chuckled his dimpled chuckle and kissed her, and her heart felt like it was going to fly out of her body and do a dance of joy above their heads. "If anything you'll find me that way, too."

"No chance." She threw her arms around him and he lifted her and swung her around and just like that she saw Radio City Music Hall right there, over his shoulder. It made her laugh again, kiss the love of her life and gaze into the eyes she knew in her heart she'd be staring into until death did them part.

"I know for a fact you're going to thrill me…every single day, for the rest of my life."

*Get ready to check in to the Hush hotel
in August 2005 with
KISS & MAKEUP
by Alison Kent.
Here's a sneak preview...*

1

To SHANDI FOSSEY, the sky was the limit, and if there was one thing she missed about Round-Up, Oklahoma, that was it. The sky. Pinpoints of white light twinkling in an inky black bowl. Cotton ball clouds scooped high on a pale blue pie plate. Butter spreading at dawn. Orange Julius at sunset.

The sky above Manhattan was about wedges cut between buildings, streetlights reflected in windowpanes and flashing neon colors—or so it seemed, sitting as she was, cross-legged and lights off in front of the floor-to-ceiling windows of her sixth floor West Village apartment at 3:30 a.m.

But that was okay. The wedges thing. Really. Because there were lights a whole lot brighter and much more meaningful here in the Big Apple than found at anytime of the day in any piece of sky over any part of the Oklahoma prairie.

And that was why Shandi was here, wasn't it? For the lights on Broadway as well as those off. The theaters and cabarets, sets and stages and clubs. Any of the myriad places offering canvases for her work.

Eyelids and lashes and lips. Brows and cheekbones. The slope of a nose. The line of a jaw. These were the landscapes she transformed, shaping and coloring and creating, turning the ordinary into the fantastic with her brushes and sponges, her pots and tubes and jars of colors and creams.

She leaned her upper body to the left, stretching dozens of muscles as she draped her right arm as far as she could over her head and down toward the floor. Her shift as bartender at Erotique in the hotel HUSH meant long hours on her feet at least five nights a week.

Afterward, unwinding beneath her own personal slice of what sky she could see had become her routine. She enjoyed the silence and the dark and the sense of so much life teeming around her.

She imagined patrons talking long into the night, analyzing and discussing and arguing over the shows they had seen. She pictured the ushers and hostesses and attendants waiting for the venues to empty so they could kick off their shoes along with their frozen smiles.

She thought of the actors easing out of their roles much as she eased from hers when she sat here each night, leaving behind the Shandi who mixed martinis and margaritas for Erotique's sophisticated clientele and slipping—reluctantly? regretfully?—back into the role of the long-legged, willowy cat's-tail of a filly from Oklahoma, a name she'd often been called by the beer-and-whiskey crowd at The Thirsty Rattler, her family's bar in Round-Up.

One of these days she would figure out which of the two women she was, whether she needed to make a choice between them, or combine both into one whole. Had she left Oklahoma to encouraging farewells instead of predictions that she'd return in six months, her tail tucked between her legs, she might find the marriage of her two selves easier.

For two years now, she'd been pursuing a degree in cosmetics marketing at the Fashion Institute of Technology, temping for a living—most recently at the law firm of Winslow, Reynolds and Forster—until hearing of the opening of Erotique and HUSH. She'd been satisfied with the status quo of her studies, her work schedule and her friends, needing nothing more. Or so she had thought.

Until tonight, when *he* had sat down at the bar.

She realigned her body to stretch her left side, her fingertips hovering over the hardwood floor at her right hip. Mercy, but if he hadn't been the most gorgeous thing she'd ever seen. Better even than the actor from that television show about Navy investigators who had stayed at HUSH during the hotel's grand opening.

Only this guy was real, not an elusive Hollywood fantasy. One who'd wanted to talk to her. Thankfully, Erotique had been busy beyond belief, giving her a legitimate excuse to walk away and catch her breath when their flirtation took on a sexually dangerous edge as it had so easily and so often.

At least walking away had worked tonight.

But he was a guest at HUSH, meaning the odds were that she would be seeing him again. And the bar wouldn't always be as hopping as it had been this evening. He was going to lose interest really quickly if she couldn't get her act together and keep her mind—and her self-worth—out of Round-Up.

Keeping her mind out of the gutter was an entirely separate matter. It was hard to talk to the man when picturing him naked, but that's exactly how she'd spent a good part of the night's overly long shift.

His hair was blond, or had been when he was

younger. It had darkened as if streaks from the sun had been reversed by the moon, leaving him with low lights instead of high. And it was long, a bit wavy, a leonine mane. He wore it pulled back.

His smile twinkled, his eyes twinkled, his personality, too. She'd had the best time sparring, exchanging bantering quips and innuendo. She'd appreciated his wit. Appreciated, too, calls from other patrons allowing her to step away and gather her thoughts while mixing drinks and serving.

She'd asked him what had brought him to the city and to the hotel. He'd told her it was a business trip—the business of money, music and women. She'd teased back that she wasn't much for helping him with the first two, but that she certainly knew her way around being the third.

For a long moment then, he'd held her gaze, and she'd imagined his fingers that slowly stroked his glass stroking her instead. Her body had responded, her filmy bra beneath her sleeveless black tuxedo shirt doing little good to keep her private thoughts private. He'd noticed. He'd lifted his drink, his eyes on her as he swallowed, his throat working, his jaw taut, the vein at his temple pulsing.

Blood had pulsed through her body, too. It did the same now as she remembered the way he'd looked at her. As if he wanted to strip her bare, to eat her up, to discover how well their bodies fit together, to devour her once he had. And then she wondered if he truly understood where it was he was staying. How perfect a setting HUSH made for a steamy affair.

Yeah, she mused, sighing deeply as she stretched out both legs in front of her, leaning forward to grab her toes and drop her face to her knees. A very long night lay ahead. And she was already anxious to get back to work and do it all again, to see him again. And for a simple reason, really.

He was the first man since her arrival in New York to have her thinking beyond work and school to the physical things that occurred between a man and a woman. Those things she craved. Those things she missed....

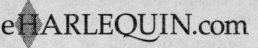

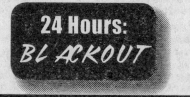

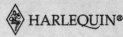

HARLEQUIN®

Blaze™

COMING NEXT MONTH

#189 INDECENT SUGGESTION Elizabeth Bevarly
It's supposed to help them stop smoking. But the hypnosis session Turner McCloud and Becca Mercer attend hasn't worked. They're lighting up even more. What a waste! Or is it? Since then, the just-friends couple has become a bed-buddy couple—they can't keep their hands off each other. In fact, it's so hot between them, why didn't they do this years ago? It's almost as if they've had some subliminal persuasion....

#190 SEXY ALL OVER Jamie Sobrato
She's going to dress up this bad boy in sheep's clothing. Naomi Tyler is the image consultant hired to tone down reporter Zane Underwood's rebel—and sexy—style. Too bad Zane is unwilling to change. Since her career depends on making him over, she's prepared to do whatever it takes...even if it means some sensual persuading from her!

#191 TEXAS FEVER Kimberly Raye
Holly Faraday, owner of Sweet & Sinful gourmet desserts, is thrilled to learn she's inherited her grandmother's place in small Romeo, Texas. That is, until she learns that her grandmother was the local madam—and the townspeople are hoping she'll continue the family business. And once she meets her neighbor, sexy Josh McGraw, she's tempted....

#192 THE FAVOR Cara Summers
Risking It All
Professor Sierra Gibbs didn't realize a speed date could lead to a thrilling adventure. Was it that earth-shattering kiss from sexy Ryder Kane that set her heart pumping? Or the fact that somebody's trying to kill her? Either way, Sierra's feeling free for the first time in her life... and she's going to enjoy every minute of it. She's going to make sure Ryder enjoys it, too....

#193 ALMOST NAKED, INC. Karen Anders
Scientist Matt Fox perfects the silkiest, sexiest material ever invented, but he knows nothing about business, even less about fashion. Yet childhood friend Bridget Cole sure does—she's a hot model with all the right contacts. Soon she's got a plan to get his material into the right hands, though first she'd like to get her hands on Matt....

#194 NIGHT MOVES Julie Kenner
24 Hours: Blackout Bk. 1
When lust and love are simmering right beneath the surface, sometimes it takes only a single day to bring everything to a boil.... Shane Walker is in love with his best friend, Ella. But no matter what he does, he can't make Ella see their relationship any other way. It looks hopeless—until a city-wide blackout gives him twenty-four hours to change her mind....

HBCNM0605